WORLDS WITHOUT END

By
CLIFFORD D. SIMAK

I0616786

ARMCHAIR FICTION
PO Box 4369, Medford, Oregon   97501-0168

*For more information about Armchair Books and products, visit our
website at…*

www.armchairfiction.com

Or email us at…

armchairfiction@yahoo.com

DREAMS CAN BECOME NIGHTMARES...

Norman Blaine worked for the Dreams Department and everyone knew he was very good at his job. The Dreams Department was supposed to give people the dreams of their choice, to put them into a world of their own choosing. It was a dream come true—literally! But when a mysterious woman dropped in on him one day, Norman discovered that something was terribly wrong. It soon became obvious that Dreams clients were not getting what they paid for, and Norman Blaine had to find out the how and why of the mystery—before it wound up costing him his life!

Here is a good old-fashioned science fiction thriller, told by one of the genre's all time greats...
Clifford D. Simak

FOR A COMPLETE SECOND NOVEL, TURN TO PAGE 89

CAST OF CHARACTERS

NORMAN BLAINE
He could give you a dream that could last a lifetime—or several. But he knew a little too much about the secrets of the Dream Department…secrets that could get him killed!

LUCINDA SILONE
This mysterious woman came to Norman wanting a dream. But what was her real purpose—to dream of another life, or to dream of exposing secrets?

PAUL FARRIS
The Protector called in to investigate a corporate murder. But he seemed bent on protecting secrets more that solving a crime.

SPENCER COLLINS
He woke from a 500-year dream, telling tall tales. Why did he run away before he could be integrated back into society?

HARRIET MARSH
Norman wanted to share her life, but she was more interested in finding a good story for the Newspaper Guild.

LEW GIESEY
The boss at Dreams. When Norman was called into his office it set off a chain of events that led to a place of nightmares.

JOHN ROEMER
Rumored to be on his way out at Dreams—and Norman might be his replacement. What dark secrets did he hold?

CHAPTER ONE

SHE DID NOT look like the kind of person who would want to take the Dream. Although, Norman Blaine reflected, one could never tell.

He wrote the name she had given him down on the scratchpad, instead of putting it on the application blank, he wrote it slowly, deliberately, to give himself time to think, for there was something here that was puzzling.

Lucinda Silone.

Peculiar name, he thought. Not like a real name. More like a stage name taken to cover up plain Susan Brown, or ordinary Betty Smith, or some other common run of name.

He wrote it slowly so that he could think, but he couldn't think too well. There were too many other things cluttering up his brain: The shakeup rumor that had whispered its way for days back and forth within the Center, his own connection with that rumor, and the advice that had been given him—there was something funny about the job. The advice was: don't trust Farris (as if he needed that advice!)—look it over well if it is offered you. It was all kindly meant advice, but not very helpful.

And there was the lapel-clinging Buttonholer who had caught him in the parking lot that morning and had clung onto him when he tried to push him off; there was Harriet Marsh, with whom he had a date this very night.

Now, finally, this woman across the desk from him.

Although it was foolish, Blaine told himself, to think a thing like that, to tie her up with all the other thoughts that were bumping together like driftwood in his brain. For there could be no connection—there simply couldn't be.

She was Lucinda Silone, she'd said. Something about the name and something, as well, about the way she said it—the little lilting tones meant consciously to give it grace and make

illustrated by FREAS

Blaine searched
through the pile of
tapes...

it sparkle—set tiny alarm bells ringing in his brain.

"You're with Entertainment." He said it casually, very much off-hand; this was a trick question and one that must be rightly put.

"Why, no," she replied, "I'm not."

LISTENING to the way she said it, Blaine could find nothing wrong. Her voice held a touch of fluttery happiness that betrayed pleasure at his thinking she must be Entertainment. And that was just as it should be. It was exactly the way that most of the others answered—flattered at the implication that they belonged to the fabulous Entertainment guild.

He gave her her money's worth. "I would have guessed you were."

He looked directly at Lucinda Silone, watching the expression on her face, but seeing all the other good points, too. "We get good at judging people here," he said. "We aren't often wrong."

She didn't wince. There was no reaction—no start of guilt, no flutter of confusion.

Her hair was honey color, her eyes were china blue, and her skin so milky white that one looked a second time to make sure that it was real.

We don't get many like this one, thought Blaine. The old and sick and the disappointed. The desperate ones and those who know frustration.

"You're mistaken, Mr. Blaine," she said. "I am Education."

He wrote Education on the scratch pad, and said, "It may have been the name. It's a very good name. Easy to say. Musical. It would go well on the stage."

He looked up from the pad and said, smiling—making himself smile against the inexplicable tension that was rising in him: "Although it was not the name alone; I am sure of that."

SHE DIDN'T smile and he wondered swiftly if he had been awkward. He snapped the words he'd said in quick review across his mind and decided that he'd not been awkward. When you were director of Fabrication, you were not an awkward man. You knew how to handle people; you had to know how to handle them. And you knew, as well, how to handle yourself—how to make your face say one thing while your mind might be thinking something else.

No, his words had been a compliment, and not too badly put. She should have smiled. That she had failed to smile might mean something—or it mightn't mean a thing, except that she was clever. Norman Blaine had no doubt that Lucinda Silone was clever, and as cool a customer as he had ever seen.

Although coolness in itself was not too unusual. You got the cool ones, too—the cool and calculating—the ones who had figured it all out well ahead of time and knew what they were doing. And there were others, too, who had cut off all retreat behind them.

"You wish a Sleep," he said.

She nodded.

"And a Dream?"

"And a Dream," she said.

"You've thought it out quite thoroughly, I suppose. You wouldn't come, of course, if you had any doubts."

"I've thought it through," she told him, "and I have no doubts."

"You still have time. You'll have time to change your mind up to the final moment. We're most anxious that you get that fact fixed firmly in your mind."

"I'll not change my mind," she said.

"We still prefer to assume you may. We do not try to change your mind, but we insist upon complete understanding upon your part that a change is possible. You are under no obligation to us. No matter how far we've gone, there still is no obligation. The Dream may have been fabricated and processed; you may have paid your fee; you may already have entered the receptacle—there's still time to change your mind. The Dream will then be destroyed, your fee will be returned, and the record will be expunged. So far as we are then concerned, we will have never seen you."

"I quite understand," she said.

He nodded quietly. "We'll proceed on that understanding."

HE PICKED UP his pencil and wrote her name and classification on the application blank. "Age?"

"Twenty nine."

"Married?"

"No."

"Children?"

"None."

"Nearest of kin?"

"An aunt."

"Name?"

She gave him the name and he wrote it down, with address, age, and classification of the aunt.

"Any others?"

"None at all."

"Your parents?"

Her parents had been dead for years, she said; she was an only child. She gave her parents names, their classifications, their ages at the time of death, their last place of residence, their place of burial.

"You'll check on all of this?" she asked.

"We check on everything."

HERE WAS the place where most of the applicants—even those who had nothing in their life to hide—would show some nervousness, would frantically start checking back along their memories to unearth some possible, long-forgotten incident which might turn up in the course of investigation to embarrass or impede them.

Lucinda Silone was not nervous; she sat there, waiting for the other questions.

Norman Blaine asked them: The number of her guild, her card number, her immediate superior, last medical exam, physical or psychic defects or ailments—all the other trivia which went into the details of daily life.

Finally he was finished and laid the pencil down. "Still no doubts?"

She shook her head. "I keep harking back to that," said Blaine; "to make absolutely certain we have a willing client; otherwise we have no legal status. But aside from that, there is the matter of ethics."

"I understand," she said, "that you are very ethical."

It might have been mockery; if so, it was very clever mockery. He tried to decide if it were or not, but he wasn't sure.

He let it drop. "We have to be," he told her. "Here is a setup which, to survive, must be based on the highest code of ethics. You give your body into our hands for our safekeeping over a number of years. What is more, you give your mind over to us, to a lesser extent. We gain much intimate knowledge of your life in the course of our work with you. To continue in the job we're doing, we must enjoy the complete confidence not only of our clients, but also of the general public. The slightest breath of scandal…"

"There has never been a scandal?"

"In the early days, there were a few. They've been forgotten now, or we hope they have. It was those early scandals that made our guild realize how important it was that we keep ourselves free of any professional taint. A scandal in any of the other guilds is no more than a legal matter that can be adjudicated in the courts and then forgiven and forgotten. But with us there'd be no forgiving or forgetting; we'd never live it down."

SITTING THERE, Norman Blaine thought of his pride in the work he did—a bright and shining pride, a comfortable and contented pride in a job well done. And this feeling was not confined to he himself alone, but was held by everyone at Center. They might be flippant when they talked among themselves, but the pride was there, hidden deep beneath the flippancy and the workaday approach.

"You almost sound," she said, "like a dedicated people."

Mockery again, he wondered. Or was it flattery to match his own? He smiled a little at it. "Not dedicated," he said. "At least, we never think of ourselves as dedicated."

And that was not quite right, he knew, for there were times when everyone of them must have thought of themselves as dedicated. It was not a thing, of course, that one could say aloud—but the thought was there.

It was a strange situation, he thought—the pride of work, the fierce loyalty to the guild itself, and, then, the cutthroat competition, and the vicious Center politics which existed in the midst of that pride and loyalty.

Take Roemer for example. John Roemer, after years of work, was on his way out. That had been the talk for days— the open secret that had been whispered through the Center. Farris had something to do with it, Lew Giesey was involved in some way, and there were others who were mentioned. Blaine himself, for example, had been mentioned as one of the men who might be chosen to step up into Roemer's position. Thank goodness, he had steered clear of Center politics all these years. There was too much headache in Center politics. Norman Blaine's work had been enough for him.

Although it would be fine, he thought, if he were picked to take over Roemer's job. It was higher up the ladder; the pay was better; and maybe if he got more money he could talk Harriet into giving up her newspaper job and…

HE PULLED himself back to the job at hand.

"There are certain considerations that you should take into account," he told the woman across the desk. "You should realize all the implications of what your decision means before you go ahead. You must realize that once you go to sleep, you will awaken in a culture different than your own. The planets will not stand still while you sleep; they will advance—or at least we hope they will. Much will be different. Styles will change, in clothing and in manners. Thought and speech and perspective—all will change. You will awaken an alien in a world that has left you far behind; you will be old fashioned.

There will be public issues of which there now is not the faintest inkling. Governments may have evolved, and customs will be different. What is illegal today may have become quite acceptable; what is acceptable and legal today may have become outrageous or illegal then. Your friends will all be dead."

"I have no friends," Lucinda Silone said.

He disregarded her and went on: "What I am trying to impress upon you is that once you wake you cannot step from here straight back into the world, for it will be your world no longer. Your world will have died many years before; you will have to be readjusted, will have to take a course in reorientation. In certain instances, depending upon the awakened person to some extent, to the cultural changes to an even greater extent, this matter of reorientation may take quite some time. For we must give you not only the facts of the changes that have occurred while you were asleep—we must gain your acceptance of those changes. Until you have readjusted not only your data, but your culture as well, we cannot let you go. To live a normal life in that world in which you wake you must accept it as if you had been born into it—you must become, in fact, part of it. And that must often be a long and painful process."

"I realize all that," she said; "I'm ready to abide by all the conditions you lay down."

SHE HAD NOT hesitated once. Lucinda Silone had shown no regret or nervousness. She was as cool and calm as when she'd walked into the office.

"Now," Blaine said, "the reason."

"The reason?"

"The reason why you wish to take the Sleep; we must know."

"You'll investigate that, too?"

"We shall; we must be sure, you see. There are many reasons—many more than you'd think there'd be."

He kept on talking, to give her a chance to steel herself and tell him the reason. More often than not this was the hardest thing of all that a client faced. "There are those," he said, "who take the Sleep because they have a disease that, at the moment, is incurable. They do not contract for a Sleep of any specified length, but only till the day when a cure has been discovered.

"Then there are those who wish to wait out the time against the return of a loved one who is traveling to the stars—waiting out on Earth the subjective time of the faster-than-light nights. And there are those who wish to sleep out an investment which they are sure, given time, will make them a fortune. Usually we try to talk them out of it; we call in our economists, who try to show them…"

She interrupted him. "Would ennui be enough?" she asked. "Just simple ennui?"

He wrote ennui for the reason and shoved the application to one side. "You can sign it later."

"I can sign it now."

"We'd prefer you wait a little."

BLAINE fiddled with the pencil, trying to think it out—wondering why this client should disturb him so. Lucinda Silone was wrong and he couldn't place the wrongness; yet, he knew he should be able to, for he met all sorts of clients.

"If you wish," he said, "we could discuss the Dream. Usually we don't but…"

"Let's discuss it," she said.

"A Dream is not necessary," he told her. "There are those who take the Sleep without one. I don't wish to appear to be arguing against a Dream; in many cases it appears to me to be preferable. You would not be conscious of the time—an hour or a century is no longer than a second. You go to sleep; then you wake, and it is as if there had been no time at all…"

"I want a Dream," she said.

"In that case, we are glad to serve you. Have you thought what kind?"

"A friendly dream. A restful one and friendly."

"No excitement? No adventure?"

"Some; perhaps, it might get monotonous otherwise. But

genteel, if you please."

"A polite society, perhaps," suggested Blaine. "Let's say, one much concerned with manners."

"And no competition, if you can manage it; no rushing about to beat out someone else."

"An old, established home," continued Blaine. "Good position in the community, high family traditions; sufficient income to banish money worries."

"It sounds a bit archaic."

"It's the kind of Dream you asked for."

"Of course," she said. "What am I thinking of? It will be lovely. It's the sort of thing, the sort..." she laughed. "The sort of thing you dream of."

HE LAUGHED with her. "You like it? We can change it, bring it up to date."

"Don't you dare, it's just what I want."

"You'll want to be young, I suppose, younger than twenty-nine—sixteen or seventeen."

She nodded.

"And pretty, of course, you would be beautiful despite anything we did."

She did not answer.

"Plenty of admirers," he said. "We could put in lots of them."

She nodded.

"Sexual adventures?"

"A few, don't overdo it, though."

"We'll keep it dignified," he promised. "You'll have no regrets; we'll give you a Dream you'll need not be ashamed of—one you can look back upon with a lot of happiness. There naturally will have to be some disappointments, a few heartaches; happiness can't run on forever without getting stale. There must be something, even in a Dream, upon which you can establish comparative values."

"I'll leave that all to you."

"All right, then, we'll get to work on it. Could you come back, say in three days time? We'll have it roughed out then and we can go over it together. It may take half a dozen— well, let us call them fittings, before we have what you want."

Lucinda Silone rose and held out her hand. Her clasp was firm and friendly. "I'll stop at the cashier's and pay the fee," she said. "And thanks, so very much."

"There's no need to pay the fee this soon."

"I'll feel better when I do."

Norman Blaine watched her go, then sat back down again. The intercom buzzed. "Yes, Irma."

His secretary said, "Harriet called. You were with the client, and couldn't be disturbed; she left a message."

"What did she want?"

"Just to let you know she can't have dinner with you tonight. She said something about an assignment, some big bug from Centauri."

He said: "Irma, let me give you a tip. Never fall in love with Communications. You can't depend on them."

"You keep forgetting, Mr. Blaine; I married Transportation."

"So I do," said Blaine.

"George and Herb are out here waiting. They've been slapping one another on the back and rolling on the floor. Take them off my hands before I go stark raving."

"Send them in," he said.

"Are they all right?"

"George and Herb?"

"Who else?"

"Certainly, Irma; it's just the way they work."

"It's a comfort to know that," she said, "I'll shoo them in."

HE SETTLED back and watched the two come in. They sprawled themselves in chairs.

George shied a folder at him. "The Jenkins Dream; we got it all worked out."

"He's the jerk who wants to hunt big game," said Herb; we cooked up some dillies for him."

"We made it authentic," George declared with pride; we didn't skip a thing. We put him in the jungle, and we put in mud and insects and the heat; we crammed the place with ravenous nightmares. There's something thirsting for his blood behind every bush."

"It's no hunt," said Herb; it's a running battle. When he isn't scared, he's jumpy. Damned if I can figure out a guy like that."

"It takes all kinds," said Blaine.

"Sure; and we get them all."

"Some day," Blaine told them dryly, "you guys will lay it on so thick you'll get booted to Conditioning."

"They can't do that," said Herb. "You got to have a medical degree to get into Conditioning. And George and me, we couldn't bandage a finger the way it should be done."

George shrugged. "We haven't a thing to worry about; Myrt takes care of that. When we go too hog wild, she tames it down."

Blaine laid the folder to one side. "I'll feed it in before I leave tonight." He picked up the pad. "I have something different here. You'll have to slick down your hair and get on good behavior before I turn you loose on it."

"The one who just went out?"

Blaine nodded.

"I could cook up a Dream for her," said Herb.

SHE WANTS peace and dignity," Blaine informed them.

"Genteel society. A sort of modern version of mid-nineteenth century Old Plantation days. No rough stuff. Just magnolia and white columns, horses in the bluegrass."

"Likker," said Herb. "Oceans of likker. Bourbon and mint leaves and…"

"Cocktails," Blaine told him, "and not too many of them."

"Fried chicken," said George, getting into the act. "Watermelon. Moonlight. River boats. Lemme at it."

"Not so fast; you have the wrong approach. Slow and easy. Tame down. Imagine slow music. A sort of eternal waltz."

"We could put in a war," said Herb; "they fought polite in those days. Sabers and all dressed up in fancy uniforms."

"She doesn't want a war."

"You gotta have some action."

"No action—or very little of it. No worry; no competition. Gentility…"

"And us," lamented George, "all spattered up with jungle mud."

The intercom buzzed. "The b.a. wants to see you," Irma said.

"O.K., tell him—"

"He wants to see you now."

"Oh, oh," said George.

"I always liked you, Norm," said Herb.

"All right," said Blaine. "Tell him I'll be right up."

"After all these years," Herb said, sadly. "Cutting throats and stabbing backs to get ahead and now it comes to this."

George drew his forefinger across his throat and made a hissing sound, like a blade slashing into flesh.

They were very funny.

CHAPTER TWO

LEW GIESEY was the business agent of the Dream guild. For years he had run it with an iron fist and disarming smile. He was loyal and he demanded loyalty; he dealt out sharp, decisive discipline as quickly as he rewarded praise.

He worked in an ornate office, but behind a battered desk to which he clung stubbornly, despite all efforts to provide him with a better one. To him, the desk must have been a symbol—or a reminder—of the bitter struggle to attain his station. He had started with that desk in the early days; it had followed him from office to office as he fought his bare-knuckled way ahead, up the table of the organization to the very top. The desk was scarred and battered, unlike the man himself. It was almost as if the desk, in the course of years, might have intervened itself to take the blows aimed at the man behind it.

But there had been one blow that it could not take for him. For Lou Giesey sat in his chair behind the desk and he was quite dead. His head had fallen forward on his chest and his forearms still rested on the chair's arms and his hands still clutched the wood.

The room was at utter peace and so, it seemed as well, the man behind the desk. There was a quietness in the room, as if respite had come from all the years of struggle and of planning. It rested now with a sense of urgency, as if it might have known that the respite could not last for long. In a little while, another man would come and sit behind the desk—perhaps a different one, for no other man would want Giesey's battered desk—and the struggle and the turmoil would start up again.

NORMAN BLAINE stopped when he was halfway

between the door and desk; it was the quietness of the room, as well as the head sunk upon the chest, that told him what had happened.

He stopped and listened to the soft whirring of the clock upon the wall, a sound usually lost until this moment in this place. He heard the almost-inaudible flutter of a typewriter from across the hall, the far-off, muffled rumble of wheels rushing along the highway that ran past the Center.

He thought, with one edge of his mind: *Death and peace and quiet, the three of them together, companions hand in hand.* Then his mind recoiled upon itself and built up into a tight coil spring of horror.

Blaine took a slow step forward, then another one, walking across the carpeting that allowed no footfall sound. He had not as yet realized the full impact of what had happened there—that moments before the business agent had asked to speak to him; that he was the one to find Giesey dead; that his presence in the office might lead to suspicion of him.

He crept up to the desk, his eyes riveted on the dead man. On one corner of the desk sat a telephone. He lifted the receiver and when the switchboard voice came, he said: "Protection, please."

He heard the clicking as the signal was set up. "Protection."

"Farris, please."

BLAINE started to shake, then—the muscles in his forearm jumping, others twitching in his face. He felt breathlessness rising in him, his chest constricting, a choking in his throat, and his mouth suddenly dry and sticky. He gritted his teeth and stopped the jumping muscles.

"Farris speaking."

"Blaine. Fabrication."

"Oh, yes, Blaine. What can I do for you?"

"Giesey called me up to see him; when I got here he was dead."

There was a pause—not too long a pause. Then: "You're sure he's dead."

"I haven't touched him. He's sitting in his chair; he looks dead to me."

"Anyone else know?"

"No one. Darrell is out in the reception room, but…"

"You didn't yell out that he was dead."

"Not a word; I picked up the phone and called you."

"Good boy…that's using your head. Stay right there; don't tell anyone, don't let anyone in; don't touch anything. We're on our way."

The connection clicked and Norman Blaine put the receiver back into the cradle.

The room was still at rest, squeezing out of the next few moments all the rest it could. Soon the fury would take up again; Paul Farris and his goons would come bursting in.

BLAINE stood by the corner of the desk, uncertainly— waiting, too. And now that he had the time to think, now that the shock had partially worn away and the acceptance of the fact began to seep into his mind, new ideas came creeping in to plague him.

He had found Giesey dead, but would they believe that Blaine had found him dead? Would they ask Blaine how he could prove that he had found Lew Giesey dead?

What did he want to see you for? They'd ask. How often had Giesey called you in before? Do you have any idea why he called you in this time? Praise? Reprimand? Caution? Discussion of new techniques? Trouble in your department, maybe? Some deviation in your work? How's your private life? Some indiscretion that you had committed?

He sweated, thinking of the questions.

For Farris was thorough. You had to be thorough and unrelenting—and tough—to head up Protection. You were hated from the start, and fear was a necessary factor to counteract the hatred.

Protection was necessary. The guild was an unwieldy organization for all its tight efficiency, and it must be kept in line. Intrigue must be rooted out. Deviationism—dickering with other unions—must be run down and have an end put to it. There must be no wavering in the loyalty of any members; and to effect all this, there was need of an iron hand.

Blaine reached out to clutch at the desk, then remembered that Farris had told him not to touch a thing.

He pulled his hand back, let it hang by his side, and that seemed awkward and unnatural. He put it in his pocket, and that seemed awkward, too. He put both his hands behind his back and clasped them, then teetered back and forth.

He fidgeted.

He swung around to look at Giesey, wondering if the head still rested on the chest, if the hands still gripped the chair arms. For a moment, Norman Blaine built up in his mind the little speculative fiction that Lew Giesey would not be dead at all, but would have raised his head and be looking at him. And if that were so, Blaine wondered how he would explain.

He needn't have wondered; Giesey still was dead.

AND NOW, for the first time, Norman Blaine began to see the man in relation to the room—not as a single point of interest, but as a man who sat in a chair, with the chair resting on the carpeting and the carpeting covering the floor.

Giesey's uncapped pen lay upon the desk in front of him, resting where it had stopped after rolling off a sheaf of papers. Giesey's spectacles lay beside the pen; off to one side was a glass with a little water left in the bottom of it; beside it stood the stopper of the carafe from which Giesey must recently have poured himself a drink.

And on the floor, beside Lew Giesey's feet, was a single sheet of paper.

Blaine stood there, staring at the paper, wondering what it was. It was a form of some sort, he could see, and there was writing on it. He edged around the desk to get a better look at it, egged on by an illogical curiosity.

He bent low to read the writing, and a name came up and struck him in the face. *Norman Blaine!*

He bent swiftly and scooped the paper off the carpet. It was an appointment form, dated the day before yesterday and it appointed Norman Blaine as Administrator of Records, Dream Department, effective as of midnight of this day. It was dully signed and stamped as having been recorded.

John Roemer's job, Blaine thought, the job that they had whispered about for weeks throughout the Center.

HE HAD a fleeting moment of triumph. They'd picked him. He had been the man for the job! But there was more than triumph. He not only had the job, but he had the answers to the questions they would ask.

Why were you called in? they'd ask. Now he could answer them. With this paper in his pocket, he would have the answer.

But he didn't have much time.

He laid the paper on the desk and folded it one third over, forcing himself to take the time to do it neatly. Then, just as neatly, he folded the other one third over and thrust it in his pocket. Then he turned again to face the door and waited.

The next moment, Paul Farris and a half dozen of his goons came stamping in.

FARRIS WAS a smooth operator. He was a topnotch policeman and had the advantage of looking like a college instructor. He was not a big man; he wore his hair slicked down, and his eyes were weak and wavery back of the spectacles.

He settled himself comfortably in the chair behind his desk and laced his hands over his belly. "I'll have to ask you some questions," he told Blaine. "Just for the record, naturally. The death is an open-and-shut one of suicide. Poison. We won't know what kind until Doc gets the test run through."

"I understand," said Blaine.

And thought: *I understand, all right. I know just how you work. Lull a man to sleep, then belt him in the guts.*

"You and I have worked together for a long time," said Farris. "Not together, exactly, but under the same roof and for the same purpose. We've got along fine; I know that we will continue in exactly the same way."

'Why, certainly," said Blaine.

"This appointment form," said Farris; "you say you got it in an inter-office envelope." Blaine nodded. "It was in my basket this morning, I suppose. I didn't get around to going through the stuff until rather late."

Which was true enough, he hadn't gone through the basket until 10 o'clock or so. And another thing—there was no record of inter-office mail.

And still another thing: Maintenance came around and emptied the wastebaskets at precisely 11:30; it was now a quarter of one, and anything that had been in his basket had long since been burned.

"And you just put the form in your pocket and forgot

about it?"

"I didn't forget about it; I had an applicant about that time. Then, when the applicant left, two of the fabricators came in. I was going over a point or two with them when Giesey called and asked me to come up."

Farris nodded. "You think he wanted to talk with you about your new position?"

"That was what I thought."

"Had he talked about it before? Did you know that it was coming?"

Norman Blaine shook his head. "It was a complete surprise."

"A happy one, of course?"

"Naturally. It's a better job. Better pay. A man wants to get ahead."

FARRIS looked thoughtful.

"Didn't it strike you as a rather strange procedure to get an appointment—particularly to a key position—in an interoffice envelope?"

"Of course it did; I wondered about it at the time."

"But you did nothing about it?"

"I have told you," Blaine said, "I was busy. And what would you suggest that I should have done?"

"Nothing," Farris told him.

"That is what I thought," said Blaine. He thought: *Make something out of it, if you can.*

He felt a brief elation and fought it down. It was too soon, he knew.

At the moment there wasn't a thing that Farris could do—not a single thing. The appointment was in order, properly signed and executed. As of the coming midnight he, Norman Blaine, would be administrator of records, taking over from Roemer. Only the delivery of the appointment was not in order, but there was no way in the world that Farris could prove that Blaine had not received it in the inter-office mail.

He wondered, briefly, what might have happened if Giesey had not died. Would the appointment have come through or would it have been quashed somewhere along the line? Would some pressure have been brought to bear to give the position to someone else?

FARRIS WAS saying, "I knew the change was going to be made. Roemer was getting—well, just a little difficult. It had come to my attention, and I spoke to Giesey about it. So had several others. We talked about it some; he mentioned you as among several men who could be trusted, but that was all he said."

"You didn't know he had decided?"

Farris shook his head. "No, but I'm glad he picked you for the post. You're the kind of man I like to work with. Realistic. We'll get along. We'd better talk about it."

"Any time," said Blaine.

"If you have the time, how about dropping in on me tonight? Any time at all, I'll be home all evening. You know where I live?"

Blaine nodded and got to his feet.

"Don't worry about this business," Farris said. "Lew Giesey was a good man, but there are other good men. We all thought a lot of him. I know it must have been a shock, walking in on him that way."

He hesitated for a moment, then: "And don't worry about any change in your appointment. I'll speak to whomever replaces Giesey."

"Any idea who it'll be?"

Farris' eyelids flicked just once, then his eyes were hard and steady, wavery no longer. "No idea," he said, brusquely. "The executive board will name the man. I have no idea who they'll put the finger on."

The hell you don't, thought Blaine.

"You're sure about it being suicide?"

"Certain," Farris said. "Giesey had a heart history, he was worried."

He rose and reached for his cap, put it on. "I like a man who thinks fast on his feet. Keep thinking on your feet, Blaine. We'll get along."

"I'm sure we will."

"Don't forget about tonight."

"I'll be seeing you," Blaine told him.

CHAPTER FOUR

THE Buttonholer had seized upon Norman Blaine that morning, after he had parked his car, just when he was leaving the lot. How the man had gotten in, Blaine could not imagine, but there he was, waiting for a victim. "Just a second, sir," he said.

Blaine swung around toward him. The man took a quick step forward, put out both his hands and clasped Blaine's lapels firmly. Blaine backed away, but the man's fingers held their grip and halted him.

"Let me go," Blaine said, but the man told him, "Not until I've had a word with you. You work at the Center and you're just the man I want to talk with. Because if I can make you understand—why, then, sir, I know that there is hope.

"Hope," he said, a fine spray of saliva flying from between his lips, "hope that we can make the people understand the viciousness of Dreams. Because they are vicious, sir, they undermine the moral fiber of the people. They hold the opportunity for quick escape from the troubles and the problems that develop character. With the Dreams, there is no need for a man to face his troubles—he can run away from them, he can seek a forgetfulness in Dreams. I tell you, sir, it is the damnation of our culture."

Remembering it now, Norman Blaine still felt the cold, quiet whiteness of the anger that had enveloped him.

"Let loose of me," he'd said. There must have been something in his tone that warned the Buttonholer, for the man let loose his grip and backed away. And Blaine, lifting his arm to wipe his face upon his coat sleeve, watched him back away then finally turn and run.

It had been the first time he'd ever been seized upon by a Buttonholer, although he had heard of them often and had laughed them off.

NOW, THINKING back upon it, he was surprised at the impact of his encounter with a Buttonholer—his horror that here, finally, he had physical evidence that there were persons in the world who doubted the sincerity and the purpose of the Dreams.

He jerked himself away from his reverie; there were other more important things with which to concern himself. Giesey's death and the sheet of paper he had found upon the floor—the strange conduct of Farris. *Almost,* he thought, *as if there were a conspiracy between the two of us—as if he and I had been involved in some gigantic plot, now coming to fruition.*

He sat quietly behind his desk and tried to think it out.

Given a moment to consider, he was certain that he would not have snatched the paper off the floor; given another moment for consideration, even after having seen what it was, he was certain that he would have dropped it back on the floor again. But there had been no time at all. Farris and his goons were already on their way and Blaine had stood defenseless in the office with a dead man, without an adequate explanation of why he should be there, without an adequate answer to any of the questions that they were sure to ask him.

The paper had given him a reason for being in the office, had given him the answer to the questions, had forestalled many other questions that would have been asked if he had not had the answer to the first ones.

Farris had said suicide.

Would it have been suicide or murder, Blaine wondered, if he had not had the paper in his pocket? If he had remained defenseless, would his luckless position have been used to explain Giesey's death?

Farris had said he liked a man who could think standing on his feet. And there was no doubt he did. For Farris himself was a man who could think standing on his feet, who could improvise and trim his course with each passing situation.

And he was not a man to trust.

BLAINE WONDERED if the appointment still would have come through if he'd not been there to pick it off the carpet. Certainly he was not the sort of man Paul Farris would have picked to take over Roemer's job. Would Farris, finding the appointment on the floor, have destroyed it and forged another, appointing someone more to his liking to the post?

And, another question: What was the importance of the job? Why did it matter, or seem to matter so much, who was appointed to it? No one had said, of course, that it was important; but Farris had been interested and Paul Farris never was interested in unimportant things.

Could the appointment, in some way, have been linked with Lew Giesey's death? Blaine shook his head. There was no way that one could answer.

The important thing was that he had the appointment; that Giesey's death had not prevented its delivery, and that, for the moment at least, Farris was willing to let the situation ride.

But, Norman Blaine warned himself, he could not afford to take Farris at face value. As steward of the guild, Paul Farris was a police official with a loyal corps of men, with wide discretion in carrying out his functions, politically-minded and unscrupulous, busily carving out a niche large enough to fit full-scale ambition.

More than likely Giesey's death fitted in with this ambition. It was not beyond reason that Farris might, in some small and hidden way, have contributed—if, in fact, he had not engineered it.

Suicide, he had said. Poison. Worried. Heart history. Easy words to say. Watch your step, Blaine told himself. Take it easy. Make no sudden moves. And be ready to duck. Especially—be ready to duck.

HE SAT quietly, letting the turmoil of speculation run out of his mind. *No use thinking about it,* he told himself. *No use at all right now.* Later, when and if he had some facts to go on— then would be the time to think.

He glanced at the clock and it was three fifteen. Too early to go home.

And there was work to do. Tomorrow he'd be moving up to another office, but today there still was work to do.

He picked up the Jenkins folder and looked at it. A big game hunt, the two zany fabricators had said. We gave him the works, they'd said, or words to that effect.

He flipped the folder open and ran through the first few pages, shuddering just a little.

No accounting for tastes, he thought.

He remembered Jenkins—a great, massive brute of a man who had bellowed out a flow of language that had made the office quake.

Well, maybe he can take it, Blaine thought. *Anyhow, it is what he asked for.*

He tucked the folder under his arm and went out into the reception room.

IRMA SAID, "We just heard the word."

"About Giesey, you mean."

"No, we heard that earlier. We all felt badly; I guess everybody liked him. But I mean the word about you. It's all over now. Why didn't you tell us right away? We think it's wonderful."

"Why, thank you, Irma."

"We'll miss you, though."

"That is good of you."

"Why did you keep it secret? Why didn't you let us know?"

"I didn't know myself until this morning; I guess I got too busy. Then Giesey called."

"There were goons all over the place, going through the waste baskets. I think they even went through your desk. What was the matter with them?"

"Just curious." Blaine went out into the hall and the chill of fear crept up his spine with every step he took.

He had known it before, of course, with Farris' crack about thinking on one's feet, but this put the clincher on it. This left no doubt at all that Farris knew he'd lied.

Maybe there was some merit in it, after all, though. His lie and bluff put him, momentarily, into Farris' class—made Blaine the kind of man the goon leader was able to understand, the kind of man he could do business with.

But could he keep up the bluff? Could he be tough enough?

Keep cool, Blaine, he told himself. *No sudden moves. Ready to duck, although you can't let them know you are. Poker face, he told himself—the kind of face you use when you face an applicant.*

He tramped on and the coldness wore away.

GOING DOWN the stairs into Myrt's room, the old magic gripped him once again.

There she sat—the great machine of dreams, the ultimate in the fabrication of the imaginative details of man's wildest fantasies.

He stood in the silence of the place and felt the majesty and peace, the almost-tenderness, that he always felt—as if Myrt were some sort of protective mother-goddess to which one might flee for understanding and unquestioning refuge.

He tucked the folder more tightly under his arm and walked softly across the floor, fearing to break the hush of the place with an awkward, or a heavy footfall.

He mounted the stairs that led to the great keyboard, and sat down in the traveling seat that would move at the slightest touch to any part of the coding panels. He clamped the open folder on a clipboard in front of him and reached out to the query lever. He pressed it, and an indicator winked a flashing green. The machine was clear, he could feed in his data.

He punched in the identification and then he sat in silence—as he often sat in silence there.

This he would miss, Blaine knew, when he moved up to that other job. Here he was like a priest, a sort of communicant with a force that he reverenced, but could not understand—not in its entirety. For no man could know the structure of the dream machine in its entirety. It was too vast and complicated a mechanism to be fixed in any mind.

It was a computer with magic built into it, and freed from the utter, straight-line logic of other, less fabulous computers. It dealt in fantasy rather than in fact—it was a gigantic plot machine that wove out of punched-in symbols and equations the strange stories of many different lives. It took in code and equations and it dished out dreams!

BLAINE started to punch in the data from the folder sheets, moving swiftly about the face of the coding panel in the traveling chair. The panel began to twinkle with many little lights and from the dream machine came the first faint sounds of tripping relays, the hum of power stirring through the mechanisms, the click of control counters, the faint, far-off chattering of memory files being probed, and the purr of narrative sequence channels getting down to work.

He worked on in a tense, closed-in world of concentration, setting up the coordinates from sheet after sheet. Time came to an end and there was no other world than the panel with its myriad keys, and trips and buttons, and its many flashing lights.

Finally he was done, the last sheet fluttered down to the floor from the empty clipboard. Time took up again and the room came into being. Norman Blaine sat limply, shirt soaked with perspiration, hair damp against his forehead, hands resting in his lap.

The machine was thundering now. Lights flashed by the thousands, some of them winking steadily, others running bright little sequences like lazy lightning flashes. The sound of power surged within the room, filling it to bursting, and yet beneath the hum of power could be heard the busy thumps and clicks and the erratic insane chattering of racing mechanisms.

Wearily Blaine got out of the chair and picked up the fallen sheets, bundling them together, helter-skelter, without regard to numbering, back into the folder.

He walked to the far end of the machine and stood staring for a moment at the glass-protected cabinet where tape was spinning on a reel. He watched the spinning tape, fascinated, as always, by the thought that upon the tape was impressed the seeming life of a dream that might last a century or a thousand years—a dream built with such sheer story-telling skill that it would never pall, but would be fresh and real until the very last.

He turned away and walked to the stairway, went halfway up, then turned and looked back.

It was his last dream, he knew, the last he'd ever punch; tomorrow he'd be on another job. He raised his arm in half salute.

"So long, Myrt," he said.

Myrt thundered back at him.

CHAPTER FIVE

IRMA HAD left for the day and the office was empty, but there was a letter, addressed to Blaine, propped against the ashtray on his desk. The envelope was bulky and distorted when he picked it up, it jangled.

Norman Blaine ripped it open and a ring, crowded full of keys, fell out of it and clattered on the desk. A sheet of paper slipped halfway out and stuck.

He pushed the keys to one side, took out the sheet of paper and unfolded it. There was no salutation. The note began abruptly: *I called to turn over the keys, but you were out and your secretary didn't know when you would be back. There seemed no point in staying. If you should want to see me later, I am at your service. Roemer.*

He let the note fan out of his hand and flutter to the desk. He picked up the keys and tossed them up and down, listening to them jangle, catching them in his palm.

What would happen to John Roemer now, he wondered. Had a place been made for him, or hadn't Giesey gotten around to appointing him to some other post? Or had Giesey intended that man be out entirely? That seemed unlikely, for the guild took care of its own; it did not, except under extreme provocation, throw a man out on his own.

And, for that matter, who would take over the direction of Fabrication? Had Lew Giesey died before he could make an appointment? George or Herb—either one of them would be in line, but they hadn't said a word. They would have said something, Blaine was sure, if they had been notified.

HE PICKED UP the sheet of paper and read the note again. It was noncommittal, completely deadpan; there was nothing to be learned from it.

He wondered how Roemer might feel about being summarily replaced, but there was no way of knowing; the note certainly gave no clue. And why had he been replaced? There had been rumors, all sorts of rumors, about a shakeup in the Center, but the rumors had stopped short of the reasons for the shakeup.

It seemed a little strange—this leaving of the keys, the transfer of authority symbolized by the leaving of the keys. It was as if Roemer had thrown them on Blaine's desk, said: "There they are, boy; they're all yours," and then had left without another word.

Just a little burned up, perhaps. Just a little hurt.

But the man had come in person. Why? Under ordinary circumstances, Blaine knew, Roemer would have stayed to break in the man who was to succeed him, then would have gone up to Records. But Roemer would have stayed on until his successor knew the ropes.

These were not ordinary circumstances. Come to think of it, they seemed to be turning out to be most extraordinary.

IT WAS a fouled-up mess, Norman Blaine told himself. Going through regular channels, it would have been all right—a normal operation, the shifts made without disruption. But the appointment had not gone through channels; and had Blaine not been the one to find Lew Giesey dead, had he not seen the paper on the floor, the appointment might not have gone through at all.

But the job was his—he'd stuck out his neck to get it and it was his. It was not something he had sought, but now that he had it, he'd keep it. It was a step up the ladder; it was advancement. It paid better, had more prestige, and put him closer to the top-third from the top, in fact, for the chain of command ran: business agent, Protection, and then Records.

He'd tell Harriet tonight—but, no, he kept forgetting; he'd not see Harriet tonight.

He put the keys in his pocket and picked up the note again. *If you should want to see me later, I am at your service.*

Protocol? He wondered. Or was there something that he might need to know? Something that needed telling?

Could it be that Roemer had come to tell him something and then had lost his nerve?

Blaine crumpled the note and hurled it to the floor. He wanted to get out, get away from Center, get out where he could try to think it out, plan what he was to do. He should clean out his desk, he knew, but it was late—far past quitting time. And there was his date with Harriet—no, damn it, he kept forgetting. Harriet had called and said she couldn't make it.

There'd be time tomorrow to clean out his desk. He took his hat and coat and went out to the parking lot.

AN ARMED GUARD had replaced the regular attendant at the entrance to the lot. Blaine showed his identification.

"All right, sir," said the guard. "Keep an eye peeled, though. A suspendee got away."

"Got away?"

"Sure; just woke a week or two ago."

"He can't get far," said Blaine. "Things change; he'll give himself away. How long was he in Sleep."

"Five hundred years, I think."

"Things change a lot in five hundred years. He hasn't got a chance."

The guard shook his head. "I feel sorry for him. Must be tough, waking up like that."

"It's tough, all right. We try to tell them, but they never listen."

"Say," said the guard, "you're the one who found Giesey."

Blaine nodded.

"Was it the way they tell it? Was he dead when you got there?"

"He was dead."

"Murdered?"

"I don't know."

"It does beat hell. You get up to the top, then poof…"

"It does beat hell," agreed Blaine.

"You never know."

"No, you never do." Blaine hurried off.

HE DROVE OUT of the lot and swung onto the highway. Dusk was just beginning and the road was almost deserted.

Norman Blaine drove slowly, watching the autumn countryside slide past. The first lamps glimmered from the windows of the villas set upon the hills; there was the smell of burning leaves and of the slow, sad dying of the year.

Thoughts flitted at him, like the skimming birds hurrying to a nighttime tree, but he batted them away—the Buttonholer who had grabbed him—what Farris might suspect or know and what he might intend to do—why John Roemer had called personally to deliver the keys; and then had decided not to wait—why a suspendee should escape.

And that last one was a funny deal; it was downright crazy, when you thought about it. What could possibly be gained by such an escape, such a fleeing out into an alien world for which one was not prepared? It would be like going to an alien planet all alone without adequate briefing. It would be like walking onto a job with which one had no acquaintance and trying to bluff one's way.

I wonder why, he thought. *I wonder why he did it.*

He brushed the thought away; there was too much to think of. He'd have to get it straightened out before he could think it through. He could not allow himself to get the thoughts all cluttered up.

He reached out to the dash and turned on the radio.

A COMMENTATOR was saying: "...who know their political history can recognize the crisis points that now are becoming more clearly defined. For more than five hundred years, the government, in actuality, has been in the hands of the Central Labor Union. Which is to say that the government is rule by committee, with each of the guilds and unions represented on the central group. That such a group should be able to continue in control for five full centuries— for the last 60 years in openly admitted control—is not so much to be attributed to wisdom, forbearance or patience, as to a fine balance of power which has obtained within the body at all times. Mutual distrust and fear have at no time allowed any one union or guild or any combination to become dominant. As soon as one group threatened to become so, the personal ambitions of other groups operated to undermine the ascendant group.

"But this, as everyone must recognize, is a situation that has lasted longer than could normally have been expected. For years the stronger unions have been building up their strength—and not trying to use it. You may be sure that none of them will attempt to use their strength until they're absolutely sure of themselves. Just where any of them stand, strength-wise, is impossible to say, for it is not good strategy that any union should let its strength be known. The day cannot be too far distant when there must be a matching of this strength. The situation, as it stands, must seem intolerable to some of the stronger unions with ambitious leaders..."

Blaine turned off the radio and was astonished at the solemn peace of the autumn evening. It was all old stuff, anyway. So long as he could remember, there had been commentators talking thus. There were eternal rumors which at one time would name Transportation as the union that would take over, and at another time would hint at Communications, and at still another time would insist—just as authoritatively—that Food was the one to watch.

Dreams, he told himself smugly, were beyond that kind of politics. The guild—his guild —stood for public service. It was represented on Central, as was its right and duty, but it had never played at politics.

It was Communications that was always stirring up a fuss with articles in the papers and blatting commentators. If he didn't miss his guess, Blaine told himself, Communications was the worst of all—in there every minute waiting for its chance. Education, too. Education was always fouling up the detail, and what a bunch of creeps!

HE SHOOK his head, thinking of how lucky he was to be with Dreams—not to have to feel a sense of guilt when the rumors came around. You could be sure that Dreams never would be mentioned; of all the unions, Dreams was the only one that could stand up straight and tall.

He'd argued with Harriet about Communications, and at times she had gotten angry with him. She seemed to have the stubborn notion that Communications was the union that had the best public service record and the cleanest slate.

It was natural, of course, Blaine admitted, that one should think his own particular union was all right. Unions were the only loyally to which a man could cling. Once, long ago, there had been nations and the love of one's own nation was known as patriotism. But now the unions had taken their place.

He drove into the valley that wound among the hills, and finally turned off the highway and followed the winding road that climbed into the hills.

Dinner would be waiting and Ansel would be cross (he was a cranky robot at the best). Philo would be waiting for him at the gate and they'd ride in together.

He passed Harriet's house and stared briefly at it, set well back among the trees, but there were no lights. Harriet wasn't home. An assignment, she had said—an interview with someone.

HE TURNED IN at his own gate and Philo was there, barking out his heart. Norman Blaine slowed the car and the dog jumped in, reached up to nuzzle his master's cheek just once, then settled sedately in the seat while they wheeled around the drive to stop before the house.

Philo leaped out quickly and Blaine got out more slowly. It had been a tiring day, he told himself. Now that he was home, he suddenly was tired.

He stood for a moment, looking at the house. It was a good house, he thought; a good place for a family—if he ever could persuade Harriet to give up her news career.

A voice said: "All right. You can turn around now. And take it easy; don't try any funny stuff."

Slowly Blaine turned. A man stood beside the car in the gathering dusk. He held a glinting object in his hand and he said, "There's nothing to be afraid of; I don't intend you any harm. Just don't get gay about it."

The man's clothes were wrong; they seemed to be some sort of uniform. And his words were wrong. The inflection was a bit off color, concise and crisp, lacking the slurring of one word into another, which marked the language. And the phrases—*funny stuff; don't get gay.*

"This is a gun I have. No monkey business, please."

Monkey business.

"You are the man who escaped," said Blaine.

"That I am."

"But how…"

"I rode all the way with you. Hung underneath the car; those dumb cops didn't think to look."

THE MAN shrugged. "I regretted it once or twice. You drove further than I hoped. I almost let go a time or two."

"But me? Why did you…"

"Not you, mister; anyone at all. It was a way to hide—a means to get away."

"I don't read you," Blaine told him. "You could have made a clean break; you could have let go at the gate. The car was going slow then. You could have sneaked away right now. I'd never noticed you."

"And been picked up as soon as I showed myself. The clothes are a giveaway. So is my speech. Then there's my eating habits, and maybe even the way I walk. I would stick out like a bandaged thumb."

"I see," said Blaine. "All right, then; put up the gun. You must be hungry. We'll go in and eat."

The man put away the gun. He patted his pocket. "I still have it, and I can get it fast. Don't try any swifties."

"Okay," said Blaine. "No swifties." Thinking: Picturesque. *Swifties.* Never heard the word. But it had a meaning; there could be no doubt of that.

"By the way, how did you get that gun?"

"That's something," said the man, "I'm not telling you."

CHAPTER SIX

HIS NAME, the fugitive said, was Spencer Collins. He'd been in suspension for five hundred years; he'd come out of it just a month before. Physically, he said, he was as good a man as ever—fifty-five and well preserved. He'd paid attention to himself all his life—had eaten right, hadn't gone without sleep, had exercised both mind and body, knew something about psychosomatics.

"I'll say this for your outfit," he told Blaine, "you know how to take care of a sleeper's body. I was a little gaunt when I came out; a little weak; but there'd been no deterioration."

Norman Blaine chuckled. "We're at work at it constantly. I don't know anything about it, of course, but the biology boys are at it all the time—it's a continuing problem with them. A practical problem. During your five hundred years you probably were shifted a dozen times or more—to a better receptacle each time, with improvements in the operation. You got the benefit of the new improvements as soon as we worked them out."

Collins had been a professor of sociology, he said, and he'd evolved a theory. "You'll excuse me if I don't go into what it was."

"Why, certainly," said Blaine.

"It's not of too much interest except to the academic mind. I presume you're not an academic mind."

"I suppose I'm not."

"It involved long-term social development," Collins told him. "I figured that five hundred years should show some indication of whether I had been right or wrong. I was curious. It's rough to figure out a thing, then up and die without ever knowing if it comes true or not."

"I can understand."

"If you doubt me in any detail, you can check the record."

"I don't doubt a word of it," said Blaine.

"You are used to screwball cases."

"Screwball?"

"Loopy, crazy."

"I see many screwball cases," Blaine assured him.

But nothing quite so screwball as this, he thought. Nothing quite so crazy as sitting on the patio beneath the autumn stars, on his own home acres, talking to a man five centuries out of time. If he were in Readjustment, of course, he'd be accustomed to it, would not think it strange at all; Readjustment worked continually with cases just like this.

COLLINS WAS fascinating. His inflection betrayed the change in the spoken language, and there were those slang words always cropping up—idioms of the past that had somehow mis-fired and found no place within the living language, although many others had survived.

At dinner there had been dishes the man had tackled with distrust, others that he'd eaten with disgust showing on his face, yet too polite to refuse them outright—determined, perhaps, to do his best to fit into the culture in which he found himself.

There were certain little mannerisms and affectations that seemed pointless now; performed too often, they could become distinctly irritating. These were actions like stroking his chin when he was thinking, or popping joints by pulling at his fingers. That last one, Blaine told himself, was unnerving and indecent. Perhaps in the past it had not been ill bred to fiddle with one's body. He'd have to look that one up, he told himself, or maybe ask someone. The boys in

Readjustment would know—they'd know a lot of things.

"I wonder if you'd tell me," Blaine asked, "this theory of yours. Did it work out the way you thought it would?"

"I don't know. You'll agree, perhaps, that I've scarcely been in a position to find out."

"I suppose that's true. But I thought you might have asked."

"I didn't ask," said Collins.

THEY SAT in the evening silence, looking out across the valley.

"You've come a long way in the last five hundred years," Collins finally said. "When I went to sleep, we were speculating on the stars and everyone was saying that the light speed limit had us licked on that. But today—"

"I know," said Blaine. "Another five hundred years..."

"You could go on forever and forever—sleep a thousand years and see what had happened. Then another..."

"It wouldn't be worth it."

"You're telling me," said Collins.

A nighthawk skimmed above the trees and planed into the sky in jerky, fluttering motions, busy catching insects. "That doesn't change," said Collins. "I can remember nighthawks..."

He paused, then asked. "What are you going to do with me?"

"You're my guest."

"Until the keepers come."

"We'll talk about it later; you are safe tonight."

"There is one thing you've been wondering about; I've watched it gnawing at you."

"Why you ran away."

"That is it," said Collins.

"Well?"

"I chose a dream," said Collins, "such as you might expect. I asked a professorial retreat—a sort of idealized monastery where I could spend my time in study, where I could live with other men who could talk my language. I wanted peace—a walk along a quiet river, a good sunset, simple food, time for reading and for thinking…"

BLAINE NODDED appreciatively. "A good choice, Collins; there should be more like it."

"I thought so, too," said Collins. "It was what I wanted."

"It proved enjoyable?"

"I wouldn't know."

"Wouldn't know?"

"I never got it."

"But the Dream was fabricated…"

"I got a different dream."

"There was some mistake."

"No mistake," said Collins; "I am sure there wasn't."

"When you ask for a certain dream," Blaine began, speaking stiffly. However, Collins cut him short.

"There was no mistake, I tell you. The dream was substituted."

"How could you know that?"

"Because the dream they gave me wasn't one that anyone would ask for. Not even one that ever would be thought of. It was one that was deliberately tailored for some reason I can't figure out. It was a different world."

"An alien world!"

"Not alien; it was Earth, all right—but a different culture. I lived five hundred years in that world, every minute of five hundred years. The dream pattern was not shortened as I understand they often are, telescoping a thousand years of Sleep into a normal lifetime. I got the works, the full five hundred years. I know what the score is when I tell you that it was a deliberately fashioned dream—no mistake at all—but fashioned for a purpose."

"Now let's not rush ahead so fast," protested Blaine. "Let us take it easy. The world had a different culture?"

"It was a world," said Collins, "in which the profit motive had been eliminated, in which the concept of profit never had been thought of. It was the same world that we have, but locking in all the factors and forces that in our world stem from the profit motive. To me, of course, it was utterly fantastic, but to the natives of the place—if you can call them that—it seemed the normal thing."

HE WATCHED Blaine closely. "I think you'll agree," he said, "that no one would want to live in a world like that. No one would ask a Dream like that."

"Some economist, perhaps…"

"An economist would know better. And, aside from that, there was a terribly consistent pattern to the dream that no one without prior knowledge could ever figure out to put into a dream."

"Our machine…"

"Your machine would have no more prior knowledge than you yourself. No more, at least, than your best economist. And another thing—that machine is illogical; that's the beauty of it. It needn't think in logic. It shouldn't, because that would spoil the Dream. A Dream should not be logical."

"And yours was logical?"

"Very logical," said Collins. "You can figure out the factors hell to breakfast and you can't tell what will happen until you see a thing in action. That is logic for you."

He rose and walked across the patio, then walked back again, stood facing Blaine. "That's why I ran away. There's something dirty going on; I can't trust that gang of yours."

"I don't know," said Blaine. "I simply do not know."

"I can clear out if you want me to; no need to get yourself messed up in a deal like this. You took me in and fed me, gave me clothes, and you listened to me. I don't know how far I can get, but…"

"No," said Blaine, "you're staying here. This is something that needs investigation, and I may need you later on. Keep out of sight. Don't mind the robots. We can trust them; they won't talk."

"If they smell me out," said Collins, "I'll manage to get off your land before they nab me. Caught, I'll keep my mouth shut."

Norman Blaine rose slowly and held out his hand. Collins took it in a swift, sure grip. "It's a deal."

"It's a deal," echoed Blaine.

CHAPTER SEVEN

AT NIGHT, the Center was a place of ghosts, its deserted corridors ringing with their emptiness. Men worked throughout the building, Blaine knew—the Readjustment force; the Conditioners; the Tank Room gang, but there was no sign of them.

A robot guard stepped out of his embrasure. "Who goes there?"

"Blaine. Norman Blaine."

The robot stood for a second, whirring gently, searching through its memory banks to find the name of Blaine. "Identification," it said.

Blaine held up his identification disk. "Pass, Blaine," the robot said, then tried an amenity. "Working late?"

"Something I forgot," Blaine told it.

He went along the corridor and took the elevator, got out at the sixth.

Another robot stopped him. He identified himself.

"You're on the wrong floor, Blaine."

"New appointment." He showed the robot the form.

"All right, Blaine," it said.

BLAINE WENT along the corridor and found the door to Records. He tried six keys before he hit the right one and the door swung open.

He closed the door behind him and waited until he could see a little before he found the light switch.

There was a front office; off it, a door led into the record stacks. What he sought should be here somewhere, Blaine told himself. Myrt would have finished it hours before—the Jenkins dream of big game shooting in the steaming jungle.

It would not have been filed as yet, might not be filed at all, for Jenkins would be coming in to take the Sleep in just a day or two. Perhaps there was a rack somewhere where the dreams-to-be-called-for were placed against their use.

He walked around a desk and looked about the room. Filing cabinets, more desks, a testing cubicle, a drink and lunch dispenser, and a rack in which were stacked half a dozen reels.

He walked swiftly to the rack and picked up the first reel. He found the Jenkins Dream five reels down and stood with it in his hand, wondering just how insane a man could get.

Collins must be mistaken, or there had been some mistake—or it was all a lie, directed to what purpose he had no idea. It simply couldn't be, Blaine told himself, that a dream would be deliberately substituted.

But he had come this far. Thus far he had a made a fool out of himself...

He shrugged; he might just as well go all the way now that he was here.

REEL IN hand, Norman Blaine walked into the testing

cubicle and closed the door behind him. He inserted the reel and set the time at thirty minutes; then he put the cap upon his head and lay down upon the bed. Reaching out, he turned on the mechanism.

There was a faint whirring of the mechanism. Something puffed into his face and the whirr noise was gone; the cubicle was gone and Blaine stood in a desert, or what seemed to be a desert.

The landscape was red and yellow; there was a sun, and heat rose up from sand and rocks to strike him in the face. He raised his head to stare out at the horizons and saw that they lay far distant, for the land was flat. A lizard ran, squeaking, from the shade of one rock to the shadow of another. Far in the hot silk-blue of the sky a bird was circling.

He saw that he stood upon a road of sorts; it wound across the desert's face until it was lost in the heat-waves that rose up from the tortured ground. And far off on the road a black speck traveled slowly.

He looked around for shade and there was no shade, nothing big enough to cast a shadow for anything bigger than the scuttling, squeaking lizard;

Blaine lifted his bands and looked at them; they were tanned so deeply, that for a moment, he thought that they were black. He wore a pair of ragged trousers, chewed off between knee and ankle and a tattered shirt, plastered to his back with sweat. He wore no shoes, and wondered about that until he lifted his feet and saw the horn-like calluses that had grown upon them to protect them from the heat and rocks.

WONDERING dimly what he might be doing here, what he had been doing a moment before, what he was supposed to do, Norman Blaine stood and stared off across the desert.

There was not a thing to see—dust, the red and yellow, and the sand and heat.

He shuffled his feet in the sand, digging holes with his toes, then smoothing then out again with the flat of his callused feet. Then the memory of who he was, and what he had meant to do, came seeping slowly back. It came in snatches and in driblets, and a great deal of it did not seem to make much sense.

He had left his home village that morning to travel to a city. There was some important reason why he should make the trip, although for the life of him he could not think of the reason. He had come from thataway and he was going thisaway; he wished that he could at least remember the name of his home village. It would be embarrassing if he met someone who asked him where he hailed from, and he could not tell them. He wished, too, that he could remember the name of the city he was going to, but that didn't matter quite so much. After a time, he'd get there and learn the name.

HE STARTED down the road, going thisaway, and be seemed to remember that he had a long way to travel yet. Somehow or other, he'd fooled around and lost a lot of time; it behooved him to get a hustle on if he expected to reach the city before nightfall.

He saw the black dot moving on the road and now it seemed much closer.

He was not afraid of the black dot and that was encouraging, he told himself. But when he tried to figure out why it should be so encouraging, Blaine simply couldn't say.

And because he had wasted a lot of time and had a long way yet to go, he broke into a trot. He legged it down the road as fast as he could go, despite the roughness of the trail and the hotness of the sun. As he ran he slapped his pockets and found that in one of them he carried certain objects. He knew immediately that the objects were of more than ordinary value; in a little while, he'd know what the objects were.

The black dot drew nearer; finally, it was close enough so that Blaine could see it was a large cart with wooden wheels. It was drawn by a flyblown camel; a man sat upon the seat of the cart, beneath a tattered umbrella that, at one time, might have been colorful but now was bleached by the sun to a filthy gray.

He approached the cart, still running, and finally drew abreast of it. The man yelled something at the camel, which stopped.

"You took your time," he said. "Now get up here; get a wiggle on."

"I was detained," said Blaine.

"You were detained," sneered the other man, and thrust the reins at Blaine, jumping off the cart.

Blaine yelled at the camel and slapped him with the reins; he wondered what in hell was going on, and he was back in the cubicle again. His shirt was stuck against his back with perspiration, and he could feel the heat of the desert sun fading from his face.

HE LAY for a long moment, gathering his wits, reorienting himself. Beside him the reel moved slowly, bunching up the tape against the helmet slot. Blaine reached out a hand and stopped it, slowly spun it backwards to take up the tape.

There the horror of it dawned upon him, and for a moment he was afraid that he might cry out; but the cry died in his throat and he lay there motionless, frozen with the realization of what had happened.

He swung his feet off the cot and jerked the reel from its holder, stripping the tape out of the helmet. He turned the reel on its side and read the number and the name. The name was Jenkins, and the number was the identifying code he'd punched into the dream machine that very afternoon. There could be no mistake about it. The reel held the Jenkins dream. It was the reel that would be sent down in another day or two, when Jenkins came to take the sleep.

And Jenkins, who had hankered for a big-game hunting trip, who had wanted to spend the next two hundreds years on a shooting orgy, would find himself standing in a red and yellow desert on a track that could be called a road only by the utmost courtesy; in the distance he would see a moving dot, that would turn out later to be a camel and a chart.

He'd find himself in a desert with ragged pants and tattered shirt and with something in his pocket of more than ordinary value—but there would be no jungles and no veldt; there'd be no guns and no safari. There'd be no hunting trip at all.

How many others? Blaine asked himself. *How many others failed to get the dream they wanted?* And what was more: *Why had they failed to get the dream they wanted?*

Why had the dreams been substituted?

Or *had* they been substituted? Had Myrt—

He shook his head at that one. The great machine did what it was told. It took in the symbols and equations and it chattered and it clanked and thundered, and it spun the dream that was asked of it.

Substitution was the only answer, for the dreams were monitored in this very cubicle. No dream went out until someone had checked to see that it was the dream ordered by the Sleeper.

COLLINS HAD lived out five hundred years in a world that lacked the profit concept. And the red and yellow desert—what kind of world was that? Norman Blaine had not been there long enough to know; but there was one thing be did know—that, like Collins' world, the Jenkins world was one no one would ask to live In.

The cart had wooden wheels and had been pulled by camel-power; that might mean that it was a world in which the idea of mechanized transportation never had been thought of. But it might, as well, be anyone of a thousand other kinds of cultures.

Blaine opened the door of the cubicle and went out. He put the reel back in the rack and stood for a moment in the center of the icy room. After a moment, he realized that it was not the room that was icy, but himself.

This afternoon, when he had talked with Lucinda Silone, Blaine had thought of himself as a dedicated person, had thought of the Center and the guild as a place of dedication. He had talked unctuously of the fact there must be no taint upon the guild, that it must at all times perform its services so as to merit the confidence of anyone who might apply for Sleep.

And where was that dedication now? Where was the public confidence?

How many others had been given substituted dreams? How long had this been going on? Five hundred years ago, Spencer Collins had been given a dream that was not the dream he wanted. So the tampering had been going on five hundred years, at least.

And how many others in the years to come?

LUCINDA SILONE—what kind of dream would she get? Would it be the mid-nineteenth century plantation or some other place? How many of the dreams that Blaine helped create in Fabrication had been changed?

He thought of the girl who had sat across the desk from him that morning—the honey color hair and the blue eyes, the milky whiteness of her skin, the way she talked, the things she had said, and the others that she had not said.

She, too, he thought.

And there was an answer to that. He moved swiftly toward the door.

CHAPTER EIGHT

HE CLIMBED the steps and rang the bell; a voice told him to come in.

Lucinda Silone sat in a chair beside a window. There was only one light—a dim light—in the far corner of the room, so that she sat in shadow. "Oh, it's you," she said. "You do the investigating, too."

"Miss Silone…"

"Come in and have a seat. I'm quite willing to answer any questions; you see, I am still convinced—"

"Miss Silone," said Blaine, "I came to tell you not to take the Sleep. I came to warn you; I have—"

"You fool," she said. "You utter, silly fool."

"But—"

"Get out of here," she told him.

"But it's…"

She rose out of her chair and there was scorn in every line of her. "So I can't take a chance. Go ahead; tell me it's dangerous. Go on and tell me it's a trick. You fool—I knew all that before I ever came."

"You knew…"

They stood for a moment in tense silence, each staring at the other. "And now *you* know." And she said something else he had thought himself not half an hour before: "How about that dedication now?"

"Miss Silone, I came to tell you—"

"Don't tell anyone," she said. "Go back home and forget

you know it; you'll be more comfortable that way. Not dedicated, maybe, but much more comfortable. And you'll live a good deal longer."

"There is no need to threaten—"

"Not a threat, Blaine; just a tip. If word should get to Farris that you know, you could count your life in hours. And I could see that the tip got round to Farris. I know just the way to do it."

"But Farris…"

"He's dedicated, too?"

"Well, no, perhaps not. I don't…"

The thought was laughable. Paul Farris dedicated!

"When I come back to Center," she said, speaking evenly and calmly, "we'll proceed just as if this had never happened. You'll make it your personal business to see that my Sleep goes through, without a hitch. Because if you don't, word will get to Farris."

"But why is it so important that you take the Sleep, knowing what you do?"

"Maybe I'm Entertainment," she said. "You rule out Entertainment, don't you? You asked me if I was Entertainment and you were very foxy while you were doing it. You fob off Entertainment because you're afraid they'll steal your Dreams for solidiographs. They tried to do it once, and you've been jumpy ever since."

"You're not Entertainment."

"You thought so this morning. Or was that all an act?"

"It was an act," Blaine admitted miserably.

"But this tonight isn't an act," she said coldly, "because you're scared as you've never been before. Well, keep on being scared. You have a right to be."

She stood for a moment, looking at him in disgust. "And now get out."

CHAPTER NINE

PHILO did not meet him at the gate, but ran out of a clump of shrubbery, barking in high welcome, when he swung the car around the circle drive and stopped before the house. "Down, Philo," Blaine told him. "Down."

He climbed out of the car and Philo moved, quietly now, to stand beside him; in the quietness of the night, he could hear the click of the dog's toenails upon the bluestone walk. The house stood large and dark, although a light burned beside the door. He wondered how it was that houses and trees always seemed larger in the night, as if with the coming of the dark they took on new dimensions.

A stone crunched underneath a footstep and he swung around. Harriet stood on the path. "I was waiting for you," she said. "I thought you'd never come. Philo and I were waiting, and—"

"You gave me a start," he told her. "I thought that you were working."

She moved swiftly forward and the light from the entrance lamp fell across her face. She was wearing a low-cut dress that sparkled in the light, and a sparkling veil was flung across her head so that it seemed she was surrounded by a thousand twinkling stars. "There was someone here," she told him.

"Someone…"

"I DROVE UP the back way. There was a car out front, and Philo was barking. I saw three of them come out the door, dragging a fourth. He was fighting and struggling, but they hurried him along and pushed him in the car. Philo was nipping at them, but they paid him no attention, they were in such a hurry. I thought at first it might be you, but then I saw it wasn't. The three were dressed like goons and I was a little frightened. I sped up and drove past and tore out on the highway, as fast as I could go, and—"

"Now, wait a minute," Blaine cautioned. "You're going too fast; take your time and tell me…"

"Then, later, I drove back, without my lights, and parked the car at my place. I came across the woods and I've been waiting for you."

She paused, breathless with her rush of words.

He reached out, put his fingers underneath her chin, tipped up her face and kissed her.

She brushed his hand away. "At a time like this," she said.

"Any time, at all."

"Norm, are you in trouble? Is someone after you?"

"There may be several who are after me."

"And you stand around and slobber over me."

"I just happened to think," he said, "of what I have to do."

"What do you have to do?"

"Go see Farris. He invited me; I forgot until just now."

"But you forget. I said goons—"

"They weren't goons. They were dressed to look like goons."

For now, suddenly, Norman Blaine saw it as a single unit with a single purpose—saw at last the network of intrigue and of purpose that he had sought since that morning.

FIRST, THERE had been the Buttonholer who had collared him; then Lucinda Silone who had wished a dream of dignity and peace; and after that, Lew Giesey, dead behind his battered desk—and finally the man who had spent five hundred years in a culture that had not discovered profit.

"But Farris—"

"Paul Farris is a friend of mine."

"He is no one's friend."

"Just like that," said Blaine, thrusting out two fingers, pressed very close together.

"I'd be careful just the same."

"Since this afternoon, Farris and I are conspiratorial pals. We are in a deal together; Giesey died—"

"I know. What has that to do with this sudden friendship?"

"Before he died, Giesey put an appointment through. I'm moving up to Records."

"Oh, Norm. I'm so glad!"

"I had hoped you'd be!"

"Then what is it all about?" she asked. "Tell me what is going on. Who was that man the goons dragged out of here?"

"I told you—they weren't goons."

"Who was the man? Don't try to duck the question."

"An escapee. A man who ran away from Center."

"And you were helping him."

"Well, no…"

"Norm, why should anyone want to escape from Center? Have you got folks locked up?"

"This one was an awakened suspendee…"

HE KNEW he'd said too much, but it was too late.

He saw the glint in her eyes—the look he'd grown to know, "It's not a story," he said. "If you use this—"

"That's what you think."

"This was in confidence."

"Nothing's in confidence; you can't talk to News in confidence."

"You'd just be guessing."

"You'd better tell me now," she said. "I can find out, anyhow."

"That old gag!"

"You may as well go ahead and tell me. It'll save me a lot of trouble, and you'll know I have it straight."

"Not another word."

"All right, smart guy," she said.

She stood on tiptoe, kissed him swiftly, then ducked away.

"Harriet!" he cried, but she had stepped back into the shadow of the shrubbery and was gone. He took a quick step forward, then halted. There was no use going after her. He could never find or catch her, for she knew the gardens and the woods that stretched between their houses full as well as he did.

Now he'd let himself in for it. By morning, the story would be in the papers.

He knew that Harriet had meant exactly what she said. Damn the woman. Fanatical, he told himself. Why couldn't she see things in their right perspective? Her loyalty to Communications was utterly fantastic.

And yet it was no more so than Norman Blaine's to Dreams. What had the commentator said when he'd been driving home? The unions were building up their strength, and it was this very fanatic loyalty—his to Dreams, Harriet's to Communications—which was the basis of that growing strength.

HE STOOD in the puddle of light before the door and shivered at the thought of the story with 96-point headlines screaming from Page One.

Not a breath of scandal, he had said that afternoon. For Dreams was built on public confidence; any hint of scandal would bring it tumbling down. And here was scandal—or something that could be made to sound very much like scandal.

There were two things he could do. He could try to stop

Harriet—how, he did not know. Or he could unmask this intrigue for what it really was—a plot to eliminate Dreams in the struggle for power, a move in that Central Labor struggle about which the commentator had held forth so pontifically.

Now Blaine was sure that he knew how it all tied up, was sure that he could trace the major plot lines that ran though these fantastic happenings. But if he meant to prove what he suspected, he didn't have much time. Harriet was already off on a hunt for the facts of which he'd given her a hint. Perhaps she'd not have them for the morning editions, but by evening the story would be broken.

And before that happened, Dreams must have its story to combat the flying rumors.

There was one fact he had to verify. A man should know his history, Blaine told himself. It should not be a thing to be looked up in books, but carried in one's head, a ready tool for use.

Lucinda Silone had said she was Education and she would have told the truth. That was something that could be checked, one of the facts that would be checked automatically. Spencer Collins was Education, too. A professor of sociology, he had said, who had evolved a theory.

There was something in the history of the guilds concerning Dreams and Education, something about a connection that had once existed between them—and it might apply.

He went swiftly up the walk and through the hall, trudging down the hall to the study, with Philo following after. He thumbed up the switch and went quickly to the shelves. He ran a finger along a row of books until he found the one he wanted.

At the desk, he turned on the lamp and ran quickly through the pages. He found what he wanted—the fact he'd known was there, read long ago and forgotten, dimmed out by the years of never being needed.

CHAPTER TEN

FARRIS' house was surrounded by a great metallic wall, too high to jump, too smooth to climb. A guard was posted at the gate and another at the door.

The first guard frisked Blaine; the second demanded identification. When he was satisfied, he called a robot to take the visitor to Farris.

Paul Farris had been drinking. The bottle on the table beside his chair was better than half-empty. "You took your time in coming," he growled.

"I got busy."

"Doing what, my friend?" Farris pointed at the bottle. "Help yourself. There are glasses in the rack."

Blaine poured out liquor until the glass was almost full. He said casually, "Giesey was murdered, wasn't he?"

THE LIQUOR in Farris' glass slopped slightly, but there was no other sign. "The verdict was suicide."

"There was a glass on the desk," said Blaine. "He'd just had a drink out of the carafe; there was poison in the water."

"Why don't you tell me something I don't know?"

"And you're covering up for someone."

"Could be," Farris said. "Could be, too, it's none of your damn business."

"I was just thinking. Education—"

"What's that!"

"Education has been carrying a knife for us for a long time now. I looked up the history of it. Dreams started as a branch of education, a technique for learning while you were asleep. But we got too big for them, and we got some new ideas—a thousand years ago. So we broke away, and—"

"Now, wait a minute; say that slow, again."

"I have a theory."

"You have a head, too, Blaine. A good imagination. That's what I said this afternoon; you think standing."

Farris lifted his glass and emptied it in a single gulp. "We'll stick the knife into them," he said, dispassionately. "Clear up to their gizzard."

Still dispassionately, he hurled the glass against the wall. It exploded into dust. "Why the hell, couldn't someone have thought of that to start with? It would have made it simple... Sit down, Blaine. I think we got it made."

BLAINE SAT down and suddenly was sick—sick at the realization that he had been wrong. It was not Education that had engineered the murder. It had been Paul Farris— Farris and how many others? For no one man—even with the organization the goon leader had at his command—could have worked on a thing like this alone.

"One thing I want to know," said Farris. "How did you get that appointment? You didn't get it the way you said; you weren't meant to get it."

"I found it on the floor; it fell off Giesey's desk."

There was no need of lying any longer, of lying or pretending. There was no further need of anything; the old pride and loyalty were gone. Even as Norman Blaine thought about it the bitterness sank deeper into his soul; the futility of all the years was a torture grate that rasped across raw flesh.

Farris chuckled. "You're all right," he said. "You could have kept your mouth shut and made it stick. It takes guts to do a thing like that. We can work together."

"It still is sticking," Blaine told him sharply. "Take it away from me if you think you can."

This was sheer bravado and bitterness, a feeble hitting back, and Blaine wondered why he did it, for the job meant nothing now.

"Take it easy," Farris said. "You're keeping it. I'm glad it worked out as it did. I didn't think you had it in you, Blaine; I guess that I misjudged you."

He reached for the bottle. "Hand me another glass."

BLAINE HANDED him another glass and Farris filled both. "How much do you know?"

Blaine shook his head. "Not too much. This business of the dream substitution…"

"You hit it on the head," said Farris, "that's the core of it. We'd had to fill you in before too long, so I might as well fill you in right now."

He settled back comfortably in his chair. "It started long ago and it has been carried on with tight security for more than seven hundred years. It had to be a long-range project, you understand, for few dreams last less than a hundred years and many last much longer. At first the work was carried on slowly and very cautiously; in those days, the men in charge had to feel their way along. But in the last few hundred years it has been safe to speed it up. We've worked through the greater part of the program first laid out, and are taking care of some of the supplementary angles that have been added since. Less than another hundred years and we will be ready—we could be ready any time, but we'd like to wait another hundred years. We have worked up techniques from what we've already done that are plain impossible to believe. But they'll work; we have firsthand evidence that they are workable."

Blaine was cold inside, cold with the shock of disillusion, "All the years," he said.

FARRIS LAUGHED. "You're right. All the years. And all the others thought that we were lily pure. We were at pains to make them think we were such quiet people. We were quiet from the very start, while the others bunched their muscles, shouted. One by one they learned the lesson we had known from the very first—that you keep your mouth shut, that you do not show your strength. You wait until the proper time.

"The others learned, eventually. They took their lessons hard, but they finally learned the facts of politics—too late. Even before there was a Central Union, Dreams saw what was coming and planned. We sat quietly in the corner and kept our hands neatly folded in our laps; we bowed our heads a little and kept our eyes half closed—a pose of utter meekness. Most of the time, the others didn't even know that we were around. We are so small and quiet, you see. Everyone is watching Communications or Transportation or Food or Fabrication, because they are the big boys. But they should be watching Dreams, for Dreams is the one that has it."

"Just one thing," said Blaine. "Two things, maybe. How do you know the substitute dreams run true? All the genuine ones we make are pure fantasy; they couldn't really happen the way we fabricate them."

"That," Farris told him, "is the one thing that has us on the ropes. When we can explain that one, we'll have everything. Back at the beginning there were experiments. Dreams tried it out on their own personnel—ones who volunteered, for short periods, five years or ten. And the dreams didn't come out the way they were put in.

"When you give a dream a logical basis, instead of wish-fulfillment factors, it follows the lines of logic. When you juggle cultural factors, the patterns run true—well, maybe not true, but different than you thought they would. When you feed in illogic, you get a jumble of illogic; but when you feed in logic, the logic takes over and it shapes the dream. Our study of logic dreams leads us to believe that they follow lines of true development. Unforeseen trends show up, governed by laws and circumstances we could not have guessed—and those trends work out to logical conclusions."

THERE WAS fear in the man—a fear that must have lain deep in the minds of many men throughout seven hundred years. "Is it just pretend? Or do those dreams actually exist? Are there such other worlds somewhere? And if there are, do we create them? Or do we merely tap them?"

"How do you know about the dreams?" asked Blaine. "The Sleepers wouldn't tell you; if they did, you couldn't believe…"

Farris laughed. "That's the easy part. We have a two-way helmet. A feed-in to establish the pattern and to set up the factors, a sort of introduction to set the dream going. It operates for a brief period, then cuts out and the dream is on its own. But we have a feedback built into the helmet, and the dream is put on tape. We study it as it comes in; we don't have to wait. We have stacks of tape. We have at our fingertips the billions of factors that go into many thousand different cultures. We have a history of the never-was, and of the might-have-been, and perhaps the yet-to-come."

Dreams is the one that has it, he had said. They had stacks of tape from seven hundred years of dreams. They had millions of man-hours experience—first-hand experience—in cultural patterns that had never happened. Some of them could not have happened; others of them might have come within a hairbreadth of happening—and there were many of them, perhaps, that could be made to happen.

From those tapes they had learned lessons outside the curriculum of human experience. Economics, politics, sociology, philosophy, psychology—in all facets of human effort they held all the trumps. They could pull out economic dazzlers to blind the people; they could employ political theory that would be sure to win hands down; they had psychological tricks that would stop all the other unions dead.

"THEY'D PLAYED dumb for years sitting meekly in the corner, hands folded in their lap, being very quiet. And all the time they had been fashioning a weapon for use at its proper time.

And the dedication, Blaine thought, *the human dedication. The pride and comfort of a job well done. The warmth of accomplishment and service—the close human fellowship.*

For years the tapes had rolled, recording the feedback, while men and women—who had come in trusting confidence to seek fairylands of their imagination—plodded drearily through of logic dreams that were utterly fantastic.

Farris' voice had gone on and on and now it came back to him.

"...Giesey was going soft on us. He wanted to replace Roemer with someone who would see it his way. And he picked you, Blaine—of all men, he picked you."

He laughed again, uproariously. "It does beat hell how mistaken one can be."

"Yes, it does," agreed Blaine.

"So we had to kill him before the appointment could go through; but you beat us to it, Blaine. You're a fast man on your feet. How did you know about it? How did you know what to do?"

"Never mind."

"The timing," said Farris, "The timing was perfect."

"You've got it all doped out."

Farris nodded. "I talked to Andrews. He'll go along; he doesn't like it, of course, but there's nothing he can do."

"You're taking a long chance, Farris, telling me all this."

"NOT A chance; you are one of us. You can't get out of

it. If you say a word, you wreck the guild—and you won't have a chance to say a word. From this moment, Blaine, there's a gun against your back; there'll be someone watching all the time.

"Don't try to do it, Blaine; I like you. I like the way you operate. That Education angle is pure genius. You play along with us, and it'll be worth your while. There's nothing you can do but play along with us; you're in it, clear up to your chin. As the head of Records, you have custody of all the evidence, and you can't write off that fact... Go on, man; finish up that drink."

"I'd forgotten it," said Blaine.

He flicked the glass and the liquor splashed out, into Farris' face. As if it were the same motion, Blaine's fingers left the glass, let it drop, and reached for the liquor bottle.

Paul Farris came to his feet, blinded, hands clawing at his face, Blaine rose with him, bottle arcing, and his aim was good. The bottle crashed on the goon leader's skull and the man went down upon the carpeting, with snakes of blood oozing through his hair.

For a second Norman Blaine stood there. The room and the man upon the floor suddenly were bright and sharp, each feature of the place and the shape upon the carpeting burning themselves into his consciousness. He lifted his hand and saw that he still grasped the bottle's neck with its jagged, broken edges. He hurled it away and ran, hunched against the expected bullet, straight toward the window. He leaped and rolled himself into a ball. Even as he leaped, arms wrapped around his face. He crashed into the glass, heard the faint *ping* of its explosion, and then was through and falling.

HE LIT on the gravel path and rolled until thick shrubbery stopped him, then crawled swiftly toward the wall.

But the wall was smooth, he remembered—not one to be climbed. Smooth and high and with only one gate. They would hunt him down and kill him. They'd shake him out like a rabbit in a brush-pile. He didn't have a chance.

He didn't have a gun and he'd not been trained to fight. All that he could do was hide and run; even so, he couldn't get away, for there wasn't much to hide in and there wasn't far to run. *But I'm glad I did it*, he told himself.

It was a blow against the shame of seven hundred years, a re-assertion of the old, dead dedication. The blow should have been struck long ago; it was useless now, except as a symbol that only Norman Blaine would know.

He wondered how much such symbolism might count in this world around him.

Blaine heard them running now, and shouting; he knew it would not be long. He huddled in the bushes and tried to plan what he should do, but everywhere he ran into blank walls and there was nothing he could do.

A voice hissed at him, a whisper from the wall, Blaine started, pressing himself further back into the clump of bushes.

"Psst," said the voice once again.

A trick, he thought, wildly. *A trick to lure me out.* Then he saw the rope, dangling from the wall, where it was lighted by the broken window.

"Psst," said the voice.

Blaine took the chance. He leaped from the bushes and across the path toward the wall. The rope was real and was anchored. Spurred by desperation, Blaine went up it like a monkey, flung out an arm across the top of the wall and hauled himself upward. A gun cracked angrily; a bullet hit the wall and ricocheted, wailing, out into the night.

Without thinking of the danger, he hurled himself off the wall. He struck hard ground that drove the breath from him and he doubled up with agony, retching, gasping to regain his breath, while stars wheeled with tortuous deliberation in the center of his brain.

He felt hands lifting him and carrying him and heard the slamming of a door, then the flow of speed as a car howled through the night.

CHAPTER ELEVEN

A FACE was talking to him and Norman Blaine tried to place it; he knew that he'd seen it once before. But he couldn't recognize it; he shut his eyes, tried to find soft, cool blackness. The blackness was not soft, but harsh and painful. He opened his eyes again.

The face still was talking to him and it had shoved itself up close to him. He felt the fine spray of the other's saliva fly against his face. Once before, when a man had talked to Blaine, this had happened. That morning at the parking lot a man had buttonholed him. And here he was again, with his face thrust close and the words pouring out of him.

"Cut it out, Joe," said another voice. "He's still half out. You hit him too hard; he can't understand you."

And Blaine knew that voice, too. He put out his hand, pushed the face away, and hauled himself to a sitting position, with a rough wall against his back.

"Hello, Collins," he said to the second voice. "How did you get here?"

"I was brought," said Collins.

"So I heard."

BLAINE wondered where he was: An old cellar, apparently—a fit place for conspirators. "Friends of yours?" he asked.

"It turns out that they are."

The face of the Buttonholer popped up once again.

"Keep him away from me," said Blaine.

Another voice told Joe to get away. And he knew that voice, too.

Joe's face left.

Blaine put up his arm and wiped his own face. "Next," he said, "I'll find Farris here."

"Farris is dead," said Collins.

"I didn't think you had the guts," said Lucinda Silone.

He turned his head against the roughness of the wall and he saw them now, standing to one side of him—Collins and Lucinda and Joe and two others that he did not know.

"He won't laugh again," said Blaine. "I smashed the laugh off him."

"Dead men never laugh," said Joe.

"I didn't hit him very hard."

"Hard enough."

"How do you know?"

"We made sure," said Lucinda.

HE REMEMBERED her from the morning, sitting across the desk from him, and the calmness of her. She still was calm. She was one, Blaine thought, who could make sure—very sure—that a man was dead.

It would not have been too hard to do. Blaine had been seen going over the wall and there would have been a chase. While the guard poured out after him it would have been a fairly simple matter to slip into the house and make entirely certain that Farris was dead.

He reached up a hand and felt the lump on his head, back of the ear. They had made certain of him, too, he thought—certain that he would not wake too soon and that he'd make no trouble. He stumbled to his feet and stood shakily, putting out a hand against the wall to support himself.

He looked at Lucinda. "Education," he said, and he looked at Collins and said, "You too."

And he looked at the rest of them, from one to another. "And you?" he asked. "Every one of you?"

"Education has known it for a long time," Lucinda told him. "For a century or more. We've been working on you; and this time, my friend, we have Dreams nailed down."

"A conspiracy," said Blaine, grim laughter in his throat. "A wonderful combination—Education and conspiracy. And the Buttonholers. Oh, gawd, don't tell me the Buttonholers!"

SHE HELD her chin just a little tilted and her shoulders were straight. "Yes, the Buttonholers, too."

"Now," Blaine told her, I've heard everything." He flicked a questioning thumb at Collins.

"A man," said the girl, "who took a Dream before we ever knew; who took you at the outward value that you give yourselves. We got to him…"

"Got to him!"

"Certainly. You don't think that we're without—well, you might call them representatives, at Center."

"Spies."

"All right; call them spies."

"And I—where do I work in? Or did I just stumble in the way?"

"You in the way? Never! You were so conscientious, dear. So smug and self-satisfied, so idealistic."

So he'd not been entirely wrong, then. It *had* been an Education plot—except that the plot had run headlong into a Center intrigue and he'd been caught squarely in the middle. And, oh, the beauty of it, he thought—the utter, fouled-up beauty of it! You couldn't have worked a tangled mess like this up intentionally if you'd spent a lifetime at it.

"I told you pal," said Collins, "that there was something

wrong. That the dream was made to order for a certain purpose."

Purpose, Blaine thought. The purpose of collecting data from hypothetical civilizations, from imaginary cultures, of having first-hand knowledge as to what would happen under many possible conditions; to collect and coordinate that data and pick from it the factors that could be grafted onto the present culture; to go about the construction of a culture in a cold-blooded, scientific manner, as a carpenter might set out to build a hen-coop. And the lumber and the nails used in that hencoop culture would have been fabricated from the stuff of dreams dreamt by reluctant dreamers.

AND THE purpose of Education in exposing the plot? Politics, perhaps. For the union that could unmask such duplicity would gain much in the way of public admiration, would thus be strengthened for the coming showdown. Or perhaps the purpose might be more idealistic, honestly motivated by a desire to thwart a scheme which would most surely put one union in unquestioned domination of all the rest of them.

"Now what" Blaine asked.

"They want me to bring a complaint," said Collins.

"And you are going to do it."

"I suppose I shall."

"But why you? Why now? There were others with substituted dreams; you were not the first. Education must have sleepers planted by the hundreds."

He looked at the girl. "You applied," he said; "you tried to plant yourself."

"Did I?" she asked.

And had she? Or had her application been aimed at him—for now it was clear that he had been selected as one weak link in Dreams. How many other weak links, now and in the past, had Education used? Had her application been a way to contact him, a means of applying some oblique pressure to make him do a thing that Education might want someone like him to do?

"We are using Collins," said Lucinda, "because he is the first independent grade A specimen, we have found, who is untainted with the brush of Education espionage. We used our own sleepers to build up the evidence, but we could not produce in court evidence collected by admitted spies. But Collins is clean; he took the sleep before we even suspected what was going on."

"He is not the first; there have been others. Why haven't you used them?"

"They were not available."

"Not—"

"Dreams could tell what happened. Perhaps you might know what happened to them, Mr. Blaine."

HE SHOOK his head. "But why am I here? You certainly don't expect me to testify. What made you grab me off?"

"We saved your neck," said Collins; "you keep forgetting that."

"You may leave," Lucinda told him, "any time you wish."

"Except," Joe said, "you are a hunted man. The goons are looking for you."

"If I were you," said Collins, "I do believe I'd stay."

They thought they had him. He could see they thought so—had him tied and haltered, had him in a corner where he would have to do anything they said. A cold, hard anger grew inside of him—that anyone should think so easily to trap a man of Dreams and bend him to their will.

Norman Blaine took a slow step forward, away from the wall, and stood unsupported in the dim-lit cellar, "Which way out?" he asked.

"Up those steps," said Collins.

"Can you make it?" Lucinda asked.

"I can make it."

He walked unsteadily toward the stairs, but each step seemed to be a little surer and he knew he'd make it, up the stairs and out into the coolness of the night. Suddenly he yearned for the first breath of the cool, night air, to be out of this dank hole that smelled of dark conspiracy.

He turned and faced them, where they stood like big-eyed ghosts against the cellar wall. "Thanks for everything," he said.

He stood there for another instant, looking back at them. "For everything," he repeated.

Then he turned and climbed the stairs.

CHAPTER TWELVE

THE NIGHT was dark, though dawn could not be far off. The moon had set, but the stars burned like steady lamps and a furtive dawn-wind had come up to skitter down the street.

He was in a little village, Blaine saw—one of the many shopping centers scattered across the countryside, with its myriad shop fronts and their glowing night-lights.

He walked away from the cellar opening, lifting his head so the wind could blow against it. The air was clean and fresh after the dankness of the cellar; he gulped in great breaths of it, and it seemed to clear his head of fog and put new strength into his legs.

The street was empty; he trudged along it, wondering what he should do next. Obviously, he had to do something. The move was up to him. He couldn't be found, come morning, still wandering the streets of this shopping center.

He must find some place to hide from the hunting goons!

But there was no way in which he could hide from them. They'd be relentless in their search for Blaine. He had killed their leader—or had seemed to kill him—and that was a precedent they could not allow to go unpunished.

THERE'D BE no public hue or outcry, for the Farris killing could not be advertised; but that would not mean the search would be carried on with any less ferocity. Even now they would be hunting for him, even now they would have covered all his likely haunts and contacts. He could not go home, or to Harriet's home, or to any of the other places—

Harriet's home!

Harriet was not home; she was off somewhere, tracking down a story that he must somehow stop. There was a greater factor here than his personal safety. There was the honor and the integrity of the Dream guild; if any of its honor or integrity were left.

But there was, Norman Blaine told himself. It still was left in the thousands of workers, and in the departmental heads who had never heard of substituted dreams. The basic purpose of the guild still remained what it had been for a thousand years, so far as the great majority of its members were concerned. To them the flame of service, the pride and comfort of that service, and the dedication to it burned as bright and clear as it ever had.

But not for long; not for many hours. The first headline in a paper, the first breath of whispered scandal, and the bright, clear light of purpose would be a smoky flare, glaring red in the murk of shame.

There was a way—there had to be a way—to stop it. There must be a way in which the Dream guild could be saved. And if there were a way, he must be the one to find it; of them all, Blaine was the only one who knew the imminence of dishonor.

THE FIRST step was to get hold of Harriet, to talk with her, to make her see the right and wrong.

The goons were hunting for him, but they would be on their own; they could not enlist the help of any other union. It should be safe to phone.

Far up the street, he saw a phone booth sign and he headed there, hurrying along, his footsteps ringing sharply in the morning chill.

He dialed the number of Harriet's office.

No, the voice said, she wasn't there. No, he had no idea. Should he have her call back if she happened to come in.

"Never mind," said Blaine.

He called another number.

"We're closed," a voice told him; "there's no one here at all."

He called another and there was no answer.

Then another. "There ain't no one here, mister. We closed up hours ago. It's almost morning now."

She wasn't at her office; she wasn't at her favorite nightspots.

Home, perhaps?

He hesitated for a moment, then decided it wasn't safe to call her there. The goons, in defiance of all Communications regulations, would have her home line tapped, and his home line as well.

THERE WAS that little place out by the lake where they'd gone one afternoon. *Just a chance,* he told himself.

He looked up the number, dialed it. "Sure she's here," said the man who answered.

He waited.

"Hello Norm," she said, and he could sense the panic in her voice, the little quick catch in her breath.

"I have to talk with you."

"No" she said. "No. What do you mean by calling? You can't talk with me. The goons are hunting you..."

"I've got to talk to you; that story—"

"I've got the story, Norm."

"But you have to listen to me. The story's wrong. It's not the way you have it; that's not the way it was at all."

"You better get away, Norm. The goons are everywhere."

"Damn the goons," he said.

"Goodbye, Norm" she said; "I hope you get away."

The line was dead.

He sat stunned staring at the phone.

I hope you get away. Goodbye, Norm. I hope you get away.

She had been frightened when he'd called. She wouldn't listen; she was sorry, now, that she had ever known him—a man disgraced, a killer, hunted by the goons.

She had the story she had told him and that was all that mattered. A story wormed out of the whispered word, out of a gin and tonic or a Scotch and soda. The old, wise story garnered from many confidences, from knowing the right people, from having many pipelines.

"Ugly," he said.

So she had the story and would write it soon and it would be splashed in garish lettering for the world to read.

There must be a way to stop it—there had to be a way to stop it.

There was a way to stop it!

HE SHUT his eyes and shivered, suddenly cold with the horror. "No, no" he said.

But it was the only answer. Blaine got up, groped his way out of the booth, and stood in the loneliness of the empty sidewalk, with the splashes of light thrown across the concrete from the many shop fronts with the first dawn wind stirring in the sky above the roofs.

A car came creeping down the street, with its lights off, and he did not see it until it was almost opposite him. The driver stuck out his head. "Ride, mister?"

He jumped, startled by the car and the voice. His muscles bunched but there was no place to go, no place to duck, nowhere to hide. They had him cold, he knew. He wondered why they didn't shoot.

The back door popped open. "Get in here," said Lucinda Silone. "Don't stand and argue. Get in, you crazy fool."

He moved swiftly leaped into the car and slammed the door.

"I couldn't leave you out there naked," said the girl. "The way you are, the goons would have you before the sun was up."

"I have to go to Center," Blaine told her. "Can you take me there?"

"Of all the places…"

"I have to go," he said, "if you won't take me…"

"We can take you."

"We can't take him and you know it," said the driver.

"Joe the man wants to go to Center."

"It's a stupid business," said Joe. "What does he want to go to Center for? We can hide him out. We—"

"They won't be looking for me there," said Blaine. "That's the last place in the world they'd expect to find me."

"You can't get in," said Joe.

"I can get him in," Lucinda countered.

CHAPTER THIRTEEN

THEY CAME around a curve and were confronted by the roadblock. There was no time to stop, no room to turn around and flee. "Get down!" yelled Joe.

The motor howled in sudden fury at an accelerator jammed tight against the boards. Blaine reached out an arm and pulled Lucinda to him, hurling both of them off the seat and to the floor.

Metal screamed and grated as the car slammed into the block. Out of the corner of his eye, Norman Blaine saw timber go hurtling past the window. Something else smashed into a window and they were sprayed with glass.

The car bucked and slowed, then was through. One tire was flat, thumping and pounding on the pavement.

Blaine reached up a hand and grasped the back of the seat. He hauled himself up pulling Lucinda with him.

The hood of the machine, sprung loose, canted upward, blocking out the driver's vision of the road. The metal of the hood was twisted and battered, flapping in the wind. "Can't hold it long," Joe grunted, fighting the wheel.

He turned his head, a swift glance back at them, then swung it back again. Half of Joe's face, Blaine saw, was covered with blood from a cut across the temple.

A shell exploded off to one side of them. Flying, jagged metal slammed into the careening car.

Hand mortars—and the next one would be closer!

"Jump!" yelled Joe.

Blaine hesitated, and a swift thought flashed in his mind. He couldn't jump; he couldn't leave this man alone—this Buttonholer by the name of Joe. He had to stick with him. After all, this was his fight much more than it was Joe's.

LUCINDA'S fingers bit into his arm. "The door!"

"But Joe—"

"The door!" she screamed at him.

Another shell exploded, in front of the car and slightly to one side. Blaine's hand found the button of the door and pressed. The door snapped open, retracting back into the body. He hurled himself at the opening.

His shoulder slammed into concrete and he skidded along it; then the concrete ended, and he fell into nothingness. He landed in water and thick mud and fought his way up out of it, sputtering and coughing, dripping slime and muck.

His head buzzed madly and there was a dull ache in his neck. One shoulder, where he'd hit and skidded on the concrete, seemed to be on fire. He smelled the acrid odor of the muck, the mustiness of decaying vegetation, and the wind that blew down the roadside ditch was so cold it made him shiver.

Far up the road, another shell exploded, and in the flash of light he saw metallic objects flying out into the dark. Then a column of flame flared up and burned, like a lighted torch.

There went the car, he thought.

And there went Joe as well—the little man who'd waylaid him in the parking lot that morning, a little Buttonholer for whom he'd felt anger and disgust. But a man who'd died, who had been willing to die, for something that was bigger than himself.

Blaine floundered up the ditch, stooping low to keep in the cover of the reeds that grew along its edges. "Lucinda!"

THERE WAS a floundering in the water ahead. He wondered briefly at the thankfulness of relief that welled up inside of him.

She had made it, then; she was safe, here in the ditch— although to be in the ditch was only temporary safety. They might have been seen by the watching goons. They had to get away, as swiftly as they could.

The flare of the burning car was dying down and the ditch was darker now. He floundered ahead, trying to be as quiet as possible.

She was waiting for him, crouched against the bank. "All

right?" he whispered and she nodded at him, her face making the quick motion in the darkness.

She lifted an arm and pointed; there, seen through the tight-growing reeds of the marsh beyond the ditch, was Center, a great building that towered against the first light of morning in the eastern sky. "We're almost there," she told him softly.

She led the way slowly along the ditch and off into the marsh, following a watery runway that ran through the thick cover of sedges and rushes. "You know where you are going?"

"Just follow me," she told him.

He wondered vaguely how many others might have followed this hidden path across the marsh—how many times she herself might have followed it. Although it was hard to think of her as she was now, dirty with muck and slime, wading through the water. Behind them they still could hear the shouts of the squad of gun-slinging goons that had been stationed at the block. They soon approached the wall of one of the outlying buildings at Center. They paused next to it briefly to catch their breath, then moved quickly around the building after hearing the sound of approaching footsteps from somewhere close behind.

The goons had gone all out, Blaine thought, setting up a block on a public highway. Someone could get into a lot of trouble for a stunt like that.

He'd told Lucinda that the goons would never dream of his going back to Center. But he had been wrong; apparently they had expected he'd try to make it back to Center. And they'd been set and waiting for him. Why?

LUCINDA had halted in front of the mouth of a three-foot drainpipe, emerging from the bank just above the waterway. A tiny trickle of water ran out of it and dripped into the swamp. "How are you at crawling?"

"I can do anything," he told her.

"It's a long ways."

He glanced up at the massive Center which, from where he stood, seemed to rise out of the marsh. "All the way?"

"All the way," she said.

She lifted a muddy hand and brushed back a strand of hair, leaving a streak of mud across her face. He grinned at the sight of her—sodden and bedraggled, no longer the cool, unruffled creature who had sat across the desk from him. "If you laugh out loud," she said, "I swear I'll smack you one."

She braced her elbows on the lip of the pipe and hauled herself upward, wriggling into the pipe. She gained the pipe and went forward on hands and knees.

Blaine followed. "You know your way around," he whispered, the pipe catching up the whisper and magnifying it, bouncing it back and forth in an eerie echo.

"We had to, we fought a vicious enemy."

They crawled and crept in silence, then, for what seemed half of eternity. "Here," said Lucinda. "Careful."

She reached back a hand and guided him forward in the darkness. A glow of feeble light came from a break in the side of the pipe, where a chunk of the tile had been broken or had fallen out. "Tight squeeze," she told him.

He watched her wriggle through and drop from sight.

Blaine followed cautiously. A broken spear of the tile bit into his back and ripped his shirt, but he forced his body through and dropped.

THEY STOOD in a dim-lit corridor. The air smelled foul and old; the stones dripped with dampness. They came to stairs and climbed them, went along another corridor for a ways, then climbed again.

Then, suddenly, there were no dripping stones and

dankness, but a familiar hall of marble, with the first-floor murals shining on the walls above the gleaming bronze of elevator doors.

There were robots in the hall; suddenly, the robots all were looking at them and starting to walk toward them.

Lucinda backed against the wall.

Blaine grabbed at her wrist.

"Quick," he said. "Back the way—"

"Blaine," said one of the advancing robots. "Wait a minute, Blaine."

He swung around and waited. All the robots stopped. "We've been waiting for you," said the robot spokesman. "We were sure you'd make it."

BLAINE jerked at Lucinda's wrist. "Wait," she whispered. "There's something going on here."

"Roemer said you would come back," the robot said. "He said that you would try."

"Roemer? What has Roemer got to do with it?"

"We are with you," said the robot. "We threw out all the goons. Please allow me, sir."

The doors of the nearest elevator were slowly sliding back.

"Let's go along," Lucinda said. "It sounds all right to me."

They stepped into the elevator, with the robot spokesman following.

The car shot up and stopped. The door opened and they stepped out, between two solid lines of robots, flanking their path from the elevator to the door marked Records.

A man stood in the door, a great foursquare, dark-haired man whom Norman Blaine had seen before on a few occasions. A man who had written: If you should want to see me later, I am at your service.

"I heard about it, Blaine," said Roemer. "I hoped you'd try to make it back; I figured you were that kind of man."

Blaine stared back at him haggardly, "I'm glad you think so, Roemer. Five minutes from now—"

"It had to be someone," said Roemer. "Don't think about it too much. It simply had to come."

Blaine walked on leaden feet between the file of robots, brushed past Roemer at the door.

THE PHONE was on the desk and Norman Blaine lowered himself into the chair before it. Slowly he reached out his hand.

No! No! There must be another way. There must be another, better way to beat them—Harriet with her story; and the goons who were hunting him; and the plot with its roots reaching back through seven hundred years. Now he could make it stick—with Roemer and the robots he could make it stick. When he'd first thought of it, he had not been sure he could. His only thought then, he remembered, had been to get back to Center somehow, to get into this office and try to hold the place long enough, so he could not be stopped from doing what he meant to do.

He had expected to die here, behind some desk or chair, with a goon bullet in his body, and a shattered door through which the goons had finally burst their way.

There had to be another way—but there was no other way. There was only one way—the bitter fruit of seven hundred years of sitting quietly in the corner, with hands folded in one's lap, and poison in one's brain. He lifted the receiver out of the cradle and held it there, looking across the desk at Roemer.

"How did you do it?" he asked. "These robots? Why did you do it, John?"

"Giesey's dead," said Roemer; "so is Farris. No one has been appointed to their posts. Chain of command, my friend. Business agent, Protection, Records—you're the big boss now; you've been the head of Dreams since the moment Farris died."

"Oh, my God," said Blaine.

"The robots are loyal," Roemer went on. "Not to any man; not to any one department. They are conditioned to be loyal to Dreams. And you, my friend, are Dreams. For how long, I don't know; but at the moment you are Dreams."

THEY STARED at one another for a long moment.

"The authority is yours," said Roemer, "go ahead and make your call."

So that was why, Blaine thought, *the goons assumed I would return.* That was why they'd set up the roadblock, not on one road only, perhaps, but on all of them—so that he could not get back and take over before someone could be named.

I should have thought of it, he told himself. *I knew it. I thought of it this very afternoon, how I was third in line—*

The operator was saying: "Number, please. Number, please. What number do you wish, please."

Blaine gave the number and waited.

Lucinda had laughed at him and said: "You are a dedicated man." Perhaps not those words exactly but that had been what she meant. Mocking him with his dedication; prodding him to see what he would do. A dedicated man, she'd said. And now, here finally, was the price of dedication.

"News" said a voice. "This is Central News."

"I have a story for you."

"Who is speaking, please?"

"Norman Blaine. I am Blaine, of Dreams."

"Blaine?" A pause. "You said your name was Blaine?"

"That's right."

"We have a story here," said Central News, "from one of our branches. We've been checking it. We held it up, in fact, to check it."

"Put me on transcription. I want you to get this right; I don't want to be misquoted."

"You're on transcription sir."

"Then here you are…"

Then here you are.

Here is the end of it—

"Go ahead, Blaine."

BLAINE said, "Here it is, then. For seven hundred years, the Dreams guild has been carrying out a series of experiments aimed at the study of parallel cultures…"

"That is what the story we have says, sir; you are sure that that is right?"

"You disbelieve it?"

"No, but—"

"It's true. We've worked on it for seven hundred years—under strict security because of certain continuing situations that made it seem unwise to say anything about it."

"The story I have here—"

"Forget the story that you have!" Blaine shouted. "I don't know what it's all about; I called you up to tell you that we're giving it away. Do you understand that? *We're giving it away.* Within the next few days, we plan to make all our data available to a commission we'll ask to be set up. Its membership will be chosen from the various unions, to assess the data and decide where use may best be made of it."

"Blaine. Wait a minute, Blaine."

Roemer reached out for the phone. "Let me finish it; you're beat out. Take it easy now. I will handle it."

He lifted the receiver, smiling. "They'll want your authority, and all the rest of it."

He smiled again. "This was what Giesey wanted, Blaine. That's why Farris made him fire me; that's why Farris killed him…"

ROEMER spoke into the phone. "Hello, sir. Blaine had to leave; I'll fill in the rest."

The rest? There wasn't any more. Couldn't they understand? He'd made it very simple.

Dreams was giving up its one last chance at greatness. It was all Dreams had, and Norman Blaine had given it away. He had beaten Harriet and Farris and the hunting goons, but it was a bitter, empty victory.

It saved the pride of Dreams; and that was all it saved.

Something—some thought, some impulse—made him lift his head, almost as if someone had called to him from across the room.

Lucinda stood beside the door, looking at him, with a gentle smile upon her mud-streaked face, and her eyes were deep and soft. "Can't you hear them cheering?" she asked. "Can't you hear the whole world cheering you? It's been a long time, Norman Blaine, since the whole world cheered together!"

THE END

If you've enjoyed this book, you will not want to miss these terrific titles…

ARMCHAIR SCI-FI & HORROR DOUBLE NOVELS, $12.95 each

D-11   **PERIL OF THE STARMEN** by Kris Neville
THE FORGOTTEN PLANET by Murray Leinster

D-12   **THE STAR LORD** by Boyd Ellanby
CAPTIVES OF THE FLAME by Samuel R. Delany

D-13   **MEN OF THE MORNING STAR** by Edmond Hamilton
PLANET FOR PLUNDER by Hal Clement and Sam Merwin, Jr.

D-14   **ICE CITY OF THE GORGON** by Chester S. Geier and Richard Shaver
WHEN THE WORLD TOTTERED by Lester del Rey

D-15   **WORLDS WITHOUT END** by Clifford D. Simak
THE LAVENDER VINE OF DEATH by Don Wilcox

D-16   **SHADOW ON THE MOON** by Joe Gibson
ARMAGEDDON EARTH by Geoff St. Reynard

D-17   **THE GIRL WHO LOVED DEATH** by Paul W. Fairman
SLAVE PLANET by Laurence M. Janifer

D-18   **SECOND CHANCE** by J. F. Bone
MISSION TO A DISTANT STAR by Frank Belknap Long

D-19   **THE SYNDIC** by C. M. Kornbluth
FLIGHT TO FOREVER by Poul Anderson

D-20   **SOMEWHERE I'LL FIND YOU** by Milton Lesser
THE TIME ARMADA by Fox B. Holden

ARMCHAIR SCIENCE FICTION CLASSICS, $12.95 each

C-4   **CORPUS EARTHLING**
by Louis Charbonneau

C-5   **THE TIME DISSOLVER**
by Jerry Sohl

C-6   **WEST OF THE SUN**
by Edgar Pangborn

ARMCHAIR SCI-FI & HORROR GEMS SERIES, $12.95 each

G-1   **SCIENCE FICTION GEMS, Vol. One**
Isaac Asimov and others

G-2   **HORROR GEMS, Vol. One**
Carl Jacobi and others

IT WAS A MONSTROUS CREATURE THAT SPIRALED THROUGH THE SKY...

It floated through the dark skies of the kingdom at night—and it left a wake of death in its path. What was the secret of the terrifying lavender vine, and who controlled it? Only the King, his corrupt Prime Minister, and an elfish little frog-boy knew the real truth about the vine and its purpose. However, it took a courageous slave and a beautiful girl from Earth to bring these secrets to light and expose a nefarious web of interplanetary corruption and crime that threatened the life of the King himself.

If you love epic science fiction adventure, you'll love this thrilling novel, penned by one of the most prolific science fiction authors of the golden age of pulp magazines, Don Wilcox.

CAST OF CHARACTERS

JOE PETERSON
Once a slave, always a slave? This imprisoned American thought so—until he had a chance to become King.

KING ARVO
He had a good heart, but he was the puppet of an evil Prime Minister. Would the secret of the vine help him to escape?

MARCIA MELINDA
The plight of the kingdom's slaves was this Earth woman's passion—a passion that found her marked for death.

NITTICELLO
He lusted for power and wealth—but his favorite pastime was torture. His nefarious plans reached an interplanetary scale.

PUDGE
Who was this strange frog-like creature, and what secret knowledge did he possess of the monstrous lavender vine?

NADOFF
This jolly merchant was the one man in the kingdom who could help an Earth woman bring her dream of a slave revolt to reality.

STOBBER
Leader of the King's royal guard, he was simply a loutish brute dressed up in a fancy uniform.

THE LAVENDER
VINE OF DEATH

By
DON WILCOX

ARMCHAIR FICTION
PO Box 4369, Medford, Oregon 97504

FOREWORD

SPACE travelers will tell you all about the great capitols and industrial cities of various planets, among them the skystation of Karridonza. Many will remark upon the beauty of Karridonza, whose alabaster buildings stand white and graceful against the background of the purple mists. But few travelers can tell what lies beyond those purple mists. Very few indeed have ever heard of the "lavender vine" which floats through Karridonza Valley—that airy mysterious something whose strange powers over life and death cause even the King to tremble in his dreams...

CHAPTER ONE

As usual, the King was trying to avoid an argument, and the Prime Minister was doing his best to argue. The King was only thirty-five. The Prime Minister was fifty. Fifty and smart. Smart and clever and stubborn. It was easier to let him have his way and be done with it.

"The Earth girl is walking out on us," the Prime Minister was saying. "She's angry. She thinks we shouldn't have slaves. We

beat them too much, she says. So she's all packed and ready to go. We can't keep her."

The King shrugged and started to speak, but the Prime Minister beat him to it.

"My idea is this," said the Prime Minister. "Just for the irony, we'll use a slave pilot to fly her across to the skystation."

The King waved his hand irritably. "Haven't I already said yes?"

"Six times."

"I'll say it ten times if you like. Go ahead. Use a slave."

"You're quite sure—"

"Yes!" The King rose and walked to the window. He pretended to be absorbed in watching the storm clouds gather over the valley.

Prime Minister Nitticello followed him. "I don't think you agree with me, your majesty. You're afraid a slave will run away with the air spinner. Not likely. Not when we punish runaways with death. Or maybe you're afraid that he would try to make love to the Earth girl instead of taking her safely to the skystation. Is that it?"

King Arvo winced. He didn't care to discuss his feelings for the girl.

"There's a heavy rain coming," he said gloomily.

Prime Minister Nitticello assured the King they would beat the storm. He would personally travel down into the valley and select a slave at once. "I'll pick up the ugliest, scrawniest specimen I can find—one that no slave master will ever miss."

King Arvo looked at him suspiciously. What did he mean? The King could never tell what schemes filled Nitticello's mind. All right, let him go. Anything to have a little peace and quiet.

"I'll go at once, with your consent—your majesty."

Arvo's thoughts whirled at that statement.

Your majesty? What mock politeness this is...

King Arvo watched the Prime Minister walk down the steps to the plaza and hail his automobile. It was miserable being under the thumb of a crafty old diplomat. Small but mighty, Nitticello was more than a head shorter than the King. He was a wrinkled, wiry man with a powerful voice and a troublesome will.

"But I'm not afraid of him," King Arvo told himself. "I ought to override him every day, just for the exercise. Why do I keep yielding to him? Hmm... I wonder if the girl from the Earth noticed it."

For the thousandth time King Arvo vowed he would break this invisible bondage.

Nitticello looked back with a knowing glint, and Arvo

wondered if his own secret thoughts had been guessed. Nitticello beckoned.

"Come along. The fresh air will do you good."

King Arvo drew a painful breath. Here it was again— Nitticello's deft suggestion. Fresh air? Yes, the King thought, he did need the fresh air.

He walked down the steps and crossed the plaza as the car drew up. Nitticello got in first and he followed.

As the car drove away, the Earth girl watched from her room.

MARCIA Melinda was a long way from home. This morning the Earth somehow seemed farther away than ever. A storm had advanced across the valley and she could no longer see the purple mists. Somewhere a hundred miles or more across the way was the skystation of Karridonza. Late this afternoon a space ship would take off. Would she be aboard? Was she going to walk out on this planet without accomplishing anything?

"You're all packed, Miss Melinda," the Lady-in-Waiting said, coming over to the window. "Can you see them, Miss? I'll get you some field glasses."

The Lady-in-Waiting referred to the court car, evidently. Marcia knew that the Prime Minister and the King had quarreled over something. Something about her passage to the skystation. Now they had taken a quick ride down into the valley, but the storm was closing in on them. They stopped, turned around, and started back by way of a short cut up the slope.

The Lady-in-Waiting re-entered and handed her a pair of binoculars.

"Thank you. Do you know where they were going?"

"We had our ears to the door, Miss. The Prime Minister said he was going to pick up the most dreadful slave he could find."

"A slave? Why?"

The Lady-in-Waiting shrugged. "For spite, I guess. He's going to have a slave fly you to the skystation."

Marcia's binoculars came to a focus upon a lonely figure trudging along the road. The rain was descending now, but he couldn't be bothered. He was apparently coming to the King's fortress. He was a slave, naked to the waist like all slaves, wearing the brown belt and dun-colored trunk of the laborer in servitude. Marcia believed that he must be one of the Earthmen rumored to be among the Karridonza prisoners. A little tremble of anxiety went through her.

He was tall and broad-shouldered, and he walked with a purpose. If he had been a native, he would have worn a high narrow mane of hair straight back over the center of his head. That was the Karridonzan style.

For a moment Marcia couldn't help wondering what might happen if an American slave were assigned to pilot her to the air spinner across to the skystation.

She watched with a tremble of excitement as the car approached the pedestrian. There was another figure down there, too—something that came up out of the marsh. It looked like a child—or was it a huge frog?

Now the rains were beating down and presently the slave, the frog, the car, and the entire valley scene were swallowed up in the gray downpour.

CHAPTER TWO

JUST before the rain struck, Joe Peterson heard a familiar voice calling to him from the side of the road.

"Hi, there, slave. Don't you know enough to come in from the rain?"

Joe looked around but failed to see anyone. "Where are you?"

"Down here in the marshes." It was Pudge, as Joe had guessed. Half boy, half frog. Always popping up when one least expected. Always laughing. Always looking bright and mischievous, with his sparkling green eyes as large as silver dollars and a shiny green pair of legs with webbed feet.

"What are you doing here?" Joe asked.

"I thought you looked lonesome. But you're going to have company. Guess who?" Pudge smiled before answering his own question. "The King!"

"I'm on my way to see the King," Joe said.

"The King's on his way to see you." The frog boy gave Joe a wink. Then he turned his funny face to the cloud and opened his red mouth to catch the first big raindrops. He splashed along the marshy way chuckling contentedly. "The King," he repeated, gesturing over his frog-like shoulder. Then with a splash, he ducked under.

Through the sudden downpour Joe looked back to see the car that was almost upon him. It was sliding dizzily around the slick road. It came to an abrupt stop beside Joe.

The two important looking Karridonzan officials in the rear were shouting at the chauffeur, who was having a bad time of it, trying to satisfy both of them. Now the older of the two lowered a window and called to Joe.

"Slave! What are you doing out here alone? Running away?"

Joe made a proper bow. He brushed the streaming rain from his face and came nearer.

"Sir, I'm on the way to interview the King."

The older man gave a sarcastic laugh. "Isn't that nice? The King will be most happy. I'll wager you're one of his old playmates."

The younger man, whom Joe guessed to be King Arvo himself, wasn't impressed by his companion's joke. "What business could you possibly have with the King?"

The older man interrupted before Joe could answer. "He has no business. He's probably an assassin."

Joe meant to stand his ground. By a twist of fate he had been shanghaied from the Earth and sold to a Karridonzan slave trader many months ago. He had taken his share of physical beatings but he had never been beaten in spirit. At last he had been entrusted with a day of freedom, and he was determined to see the King. He meant to present his case, and demand in the name of justice and interplanetary goodwill that he be allowed to return to the Earth.

Now the surly words of the King's companion incensed him. But he wasn't going to let any rash answers upset his plans.

He bowed as courteously as he could, and addressed the younger man confidently.

"Your majesty—"

"So you recognize me—" The King gave a start. "How did you know?"

"I was told you were coming this way."

"You were told? No one knew I was coming. I didn't know it myself until a minute ago."

"Your majesty, may I have an appointment to explain to you—"

The older man barked an order to the chauffeur and the car plunged ahead. Joe was left standing in a spray of flying mud.

Pudge hopped up out of the marshy waters.

"Congratulations, slave. You've had an interview with the King."

THE rain roared down heavier than ever and great blasts of thunder pounded through the hillsides. The car had disappeared from view. Joe trudged on, low in spirits.

It was the thunder, he thought. Lightning and thunder always reminded him of his troubles back home. It had stormed that night when they clamped him in jail over a labor squabble. He had been a laborer, and a damned good one. He'd never thrown himself into an unjust strike in his life. But some personal enemy had seen a chance to put him through the mill. One swift surprise move and Joe found himself in jail. And that night the storm had struck. The thunder roared and Joe roared back at it. He was innocent, and by the heavens he would prove it.

Pudge was now hopping along beside him, feeling very good over the falling weather.

"What's the matter, slave? Afraid of the thunder? Oh, I

know. You're telling yourself that old story about how you got into this mess. I've heard that one before."

"The door of my prison opened and someone pretending to be a good angel told me it was time to come out," Joe muttered. "I thought everything had been cleared. But the next thing I knew I was being loaded onto a space ship. They brought me up to this God forsaken planet and sold me to the Karridonza prison."

"Just like the rain," Pudge cackled. "Spatter, spatter, spatter. The same tune over and over again."

"That doesn't make it any less true."

But Joe knew that his protests of innocence had become hollow words. And now, after this roadside clash with the King, how could he hope to win?

"Keep walking," Pudge said. Then with a gay laugh, that frog-like monstrosity hopped back to the marsh. He dived in, his green webbed feet flying after him.

Joe had lost one of his sandals in the mud and was looking for it when he heard the call of the chauffeur. The car had stalled a few feet ahead of him. They were in need of help.

"Hurry up, you damned slave. Put your shoulder to the rear and help us get out of here."

CHAPTER THREE

JOE had played in luck. His muscles had turned the trick. He was a prisoner. For convenience they had put him in a waiting room cage temporarily—but at least he was here. The warm glow of the palace lights shone down upon him. He was still caked with mud from head to foot for he had helped push the car all the way back to the main highway. What he wouldn't have given for a good shower. A drink of water would help, too. You'd think they'd be more thoughtful in a king's palace. No service. And he'd better not risk rapping on the bars.

He thought of Pudge. He looked to the marble pillars along the corridor—the very sort of hiding place that Pudge would choose. He gave a low whisper.

"Pudge...Pudge!"

One of the orange-sashed guards, standing like a statue against the wall turned a cold eye in Joe's direction. Joe gulped, fell silent, and settled back against the bars to wait. Then he came up with a start.

"Holy smoke...am I seeing things?"

It might have been a dream but it wasn't. It was a girl. And when Joe Peterson said the word girl to himself, he wasn't referring to just any female from Mars or Venus or Mercury. Here was an Earth girl—the rarest of all creatures in Karridonza. She was darned attractive, he thought. Maybe not what you'd call pretty—not a painted doll type—but a keen looking person who would make the most important travelers on any space ship sit up and take notice.

She was dressed for space travel. From her attitude, Joe guessed that she had every intention of boarding the Earthbound sky ship that would leave this very afternoon. She crossed to the table where her baggage had been assembled. She checked each item, barely nodding to the officious Prime Minister as he came toward her smiling.

"You've not changed your mind, Miss Melinda?"

"No, thank you. I'll go at once. Is my transportation ready?"

Joe thought that her face brightened a little at the sight of the King. He was bringing her a gift—an ivory jewel box. It was pretty elegant, the way he opened it and handed it to her with a slight bow.

"These treasures are for you, Miss Melinda. I hope you will not forget—" The King paused as if to suggest many things that could not be enumerated. "I'm sure you will not forget—"

The girl was shaking her head. "No gifts, please, your majesty. After all, you and I are parting as friendly enemies. My requests have only troubled you."

"You can't call yourself an enemy," the King said. "No enemies ever leave this palace alive. This is a gift of friendship."

He was forcing her to accept, Joe thought. Joe was puzzled, trying to determine the degree of sincerity back of this farewell. For now the Prime Minister was also bestowing gifts—obviously the finest of jewels from his personal treasury.

"We have failed to listen to your entreaties," the Prime Minister said, rubbing his hands together and smiling unctuously, "but these gems should convince you that you have been a most popular guest."

The air spinner, as the Karridonzan "airplane" was called, taxied onto the plaza. Joe had been fascinated by the stories of its automatic controls. It could find its way back to home base like a homing pigeon.

"You needn't send a pilot with me," the girl was saying. "Can't I cross the mists and let the spinner come back alone?"

"It is a matter of Karridonza courtesy," the Prime Minister said. "King Arvo has already arranged for one of our slaves to accompany you."

The three of them came over to Joe's cage. For a moment Joe forgot to breathe. Were they going to let him act as escort? What was the game?

THE girl gave a little gasp at the sight of him. He must have looked an awful mess. He was unshaven, his hair was uncombed, and he was cloaked in slave garb and mud. He wouldn't blame her if she were frightened at the sight of him.

But when she said, "Oh, the American," and then pressed her fingers over her lips, he caught the impression that she must have heard of him before.

She was telling him something with her eyes. She was shaking her head, a barely perceptible gesture, as if trying to warn him of some danger.

Nitticello, the sharp-eyed little Prime Minister, drew the King aside, and for a moment they consulted. Nitticello had perceived something, Joe didn't know what. But whatever it was, he got a nod of agreement from the young king. In that moment, Joe knew the plan had been changed.

"We've decided to let you go alone after all, Miss Melinda," King Arvo said. "Are you quite sure you won't need a pilot's company?"

"On second thought," the girl said, "I believe I do. If it's the custom—Karridonza courtesy and all that—and if this person can be spared—"

The Prime Minister shook his head. "No, Miss Melinda. We prefer to respect your original wish to go alone. Our very best wishes will go along with you."

And that was that. All except the farewell kisses.

It must have been the King's puzzled and forlorn look that softened the girl's heart at the last moment. She leaned toward him and gave him a kiss on the cheek. Then she turned hastily, and started to walk past the Prime Minister.

But Nitticello caught her hand. "I also respect your noble Earth customs. Do you have only one goodbye kiss to spare?" The girl drew back, then yielded on impulse and kissed him lightly on the forehead.

Joe saw one of the orange-sashed officers step forward with a cocky twinkle in his eye.

"I've heard that on Earth many things come in threes, Miss," he said as he extended his hand toward her.

Then to Joe's surprise, she whirled about and said, "The third kiss is for your prisoner here."

She stepped to Joe's cage, reached through the bars to touch his whiskered cheeks lightly with her hands, and kissed him on the lips.

When the air spinner had roared away, two minutes later, Joe was still sitting dreamily wondering what had struck him.

He looked out at the gray rain, now beating down steadily over the marble plaza, and he wondered whether there would ever be another kiss like that—ever—anywhere in the whole solar system.

And suddenly he became alert with a feeling of terror. The Prime Minister was speaking to the King.

"You don't think I meant to let all of our finest gems slip out of our hands, do you?"

What did he mean by that? The girl had gone. She had flown off into the opaque clouds.

"Of course she'll not get back to the Earth with them." Nitticello was snarling quietly and there was a murderous light in his eyes. "I had hoped the jewels might convince her to stay, and possibly change her findings regarding our slave trade. It failed. She'll never get to the Karridonza skystation alive."

And even as the little Prime Minister enunciated these brittle words he was whirling the cranks of a black machine at one of the circular windows. Joe saw the shiny cannon-shaped barrel of the instrument lift to an angle that might have been calculated to shoot a blast of fire through the rain clouds. Now he was letting automatic instruments adjust it to some unseen target.

The King was too weak in mind and too confused to do anything. He was trying to make the older man stop and explain.

"You can't do that, Nitti."

Nitticello grated through his set teeth. "How do you think I've preserved the riches of this kingdom for you all through these years? By giving away our finest gifts? This ray will do the trick in a minute. It will nip a wing off. The spinner will fall. The jewels won't be harmed. And we know what to send to bring them back to us...don't we?"

"But the girl..."

"She had her chance to work with us. Peace be to her mangled bones."

The realization hit Joe like a bolt of lightning. He tore at the bars of his poorly constructed cage. To his amazement, he sprung one of them and forced it out of its socket. He wrenched at another. It bent. That was all he needed. He thrust his head and shoulders through the opening, he writhed like an eel—and then he was out.

He dashed across the corridor. But the clank of bars had alarmed a whole bevy of guards into action. They came at him from all directions.

He dodged between two marble pillars. He kicked the first guard out of his path then ducked back so the next two collided. He leaped over the scramble. For an instant the way was clear. He raced toward Nitticello and the black instrument of death.

A silver line blazed like a stream of white fire into the dark clouds. It was death—death finding its mark through the rain.

Joe knew the deadly accuracy of the apparatus, and he knew he was too late. In his mind he could visualize the air spinner dissolving under the touch of the ray. It was an uncontrolled moment for Joe Peterson, the slave. He had seized a chair and would have flung it at Nitticello's head. But something struck him across the back. He stumbled. Then the guards were pouncing on him from all directions.

They pulled him to his feet. He fell again. They couldn't make him walk so they dragged him by the feet and dumped him in one corner of the reception room. Then they stood by with weapons ready, as if daring him to start something.

CHAPTER FOUR

JOE Peterson was in no condition to start anything. The one deeply burning hurt over the lost Earth girl was all the pain he could stand. His injured back and his bruised arms and head were nothing. It was the girl—that lovely, friendly person who had kissed him only a few minutes before.

Weakly he looked past the guards trying to see what might have happened to the King.

"Could I talk with the King?" he muttered through his swollen lips.

"The King will talk with you when he gets around to it, you damned slave," one of the guards said. "He'll read you order number thirty-three. And we'll have the pleasure of carrying it out."

Joe watched in silence. He was seeing the King in a strange light. The King was hunched down in a chair, drumming his fingers nervously on the table. He was eyeing Nitticello like an

106

anguished son who would like to give his father a lecture if he only dared.

King Arvo will fire Nitticello for this, Joe thought—if he's strong enough.

But Nitticello stared the King down.

"I did it for you and the kingdom, Arvo. I'm always looking out for your best interests. Every hour of every day. That's why we're growing rich instead of poor."

Nitticello glanced around. The orange-sashed guards stood stiffly as if they weren't hearing a word. Nitti lowered his voice and talked earnestly for several minutes. The King didn't like what he was saying.

"Riches!" The King groaned like a wounded beast.

"Riches—yes. And friendships, too. Look...we have this paper...Miss Melinda's own handwriting."

He waved a piece of parchment. It was a document the girl had signed earlier, an official document of friendship for the Karridonzans' future use. This would help clear them of any suspicion regarding the circumstances of her death.

The poor, confused, weak King. Joe saw that everything had happened too fast for him. If ray-gunning the air spinner and killing the Earth girl were all for the good of the kingdom then Arvo was going to try to see it in the best light. But he detested the thought of it nevertheless.

"Why didn't we send a slave with her?" the King asked. "At first you insisted. Then at the very last minute you changed your mind."

Nitticello lifted an eyebrow, and Joe guessed he was debating whether he should reveal his change of motives. "Yes...yes it would have been a neat stroke of irony if we had caused a slave to die with her."

"But you changed the plan."

"We, your majesty. I do nothing without your approval."

"All right, we. We sent her alone." The wrinkles around Nitticello's lips tightened. He was squirming at bit. "At the last minute it appeared that our chosen slave might be too valuable to he shot down."

"Valuable? We have thousands of slaves," the King interjected.

"This fellow is quite husky. Think how he helped us out of the mud. He's strong. Well-built. He's alert and willing. Just the man we need as an example for the other slaves."

The King wasn't satisfied with the explanation, Joe was sure. But the crafty Prime Minister changed the subject.

"Please don't worry about the jewels, Arvo. Don't worry about them even for a minute." he was speaking in a low voice, and Joe doubted whether any of the guards heard. "Tonight you and I will go below. Tonight—" Then, in a tense whisper, "the lavender vine will work its magic for us."

CHAPTER FIVE

NITTICELLO sat at the table, his hands clenched tight. His half-closed eyes followed every action of the King. Their conference had come to an end.

Outside the windows the rain was beating down mercilessly. King Arvo rose to leave the room, a blank expression on his face. He seemed to be walking in a trance as he lumbered down the corridor and slowly entered one of his private chambers.

Nitticello watched him until he was out of sight. Then he rose, walked to one of the arched doorways, and beckoned to someone out of sight.

A moment later a huge guard strode in to await the Prime Minister's orders. He was dressed in a more elaborate black and orange uniform than the other guards. "Sashes," as they were called. This, Joe learned, was Stobber, the chief of the Sashes. The wide flowing orange sash which draped over his shoulder and around his waist was adorned with circles of emeralds, so that his approach was announced by the glittering green flashes from his thick swaggering shoulders.

Joe was fascinated by the roached mane of hair over the crest of Stobber's head—a weird blend of green and orange—

doubtless dyed to match his uniform.

"Stobber," Nitticello said. "I have a delicate assignment. For all I know, this visiting slave may well be a bloody assassin, but I think we may have some use for him." Nittecello turned briefly toward Joe. "We have some business to conduct...you and I." He smiled slightly then turned back to Stobber. "We picked him up on the road. He said his master had given him leave to come to the palace. He's originally from another planet—Earth, I think. He must have been one of our prison pickups—probably for some crime abroad. Regardless, I want you to assign six of your best Sashes to me as personal bodyguards until further notice."

The six guards were summoned immediately. Acting on an order from the Prime Minister, one of them brought Joe a basin of water and some clean clothes. Nitticello stopped him, however, just as he started to wash.

"Wait," said Nitticello, peering intently at Joe's face. With the wave of an arm, he motioned the six guards to station themselves outside the room. Then he turned to Joe. "I like the looks of that mud on your face."

"Do you now?" Joe folded his arms.

"It's not quite right. But it isn't bad." Nitticello cocked his head this way and that. "I noticed something very interesting about your face soon after you arrived. That's why I didn't let you go with the girl. I can...rather *we* can use you. This is the best piece of luck I've had...rather *we've* had in years."

Joe studied his face in the mirror. Then it dawned on him, and suddenly he knew what the Prime Minister was referring to.

He had a strong resemblance to the King.

He certainly wasn't groomed like the King—by any manner or means. But he had the King's face, feature for feature, from his high forehead with wide dark eyebrows and clear blue eyes to his well-molded chin and full-muscled neck. The same straight, prominent nose, the same high angular cheekbones.

Nitticello, disregarding Joe's own unshaven stubble, was plastering a dab of mud on Joe's upper lip in the shape of the

King's thin drooping black mustache. He added a small spade-- shaped beard. Then he stepped back to study the effect. He smiled—a slightly twisted smile.

He pinned Joe's shock of hair into a single thick upright wing. He was definitely pleased. He became talkative, trying to win Joe over with a quick show of friendship. Joe didn't like it.

"The people would never know," Nitticello said. "If we dressed you up in proper attire you'd be a perfect double for the King. And after all, the King certainly needs a double. All rulers do—for the delicate situations that arise from time to time. I'm sure he'd be most grateful for your service." Then Nitticello leaned in closely. "But for the time being it will be our little secret. Do you understand me…slave?"

"I heard what you said." The pent-up anger was tight in Joe's throat.

"What's your name, slave? You have a name, haven't you?"

"A number."

"No name?"

"Why should I want a name? The girl had a name, didn't she? And look what happened to her."

"Don't be so gloomy. You're alive, aren't you? Be thankful we didn't let you fly off in the air spinner, too. It's too bad that she has had a little accident—yes, very unfortunate."

Joe's fist shot out. He did it before he thought. A short hard punch. *Thud!*

The Prime Minister caught it on the jaw. He bounced back, stumbled and fell—flat on his posterior. In his mind Joe could hear the sound of a thousand cheering fans at ringside.

The sound of Nitticello hitting the floor echoed into the corridor. Instantly six guards were in the room helping the fallen Prime Minster pick himself up, demanding to know what had happened.

Joe smeared the mud from his face, untangled his hair, and stepped back. He tightened his fists and waited for the worse. But the worst didn't come. Nitticello was looking at him curiously and for some strange reason he waved it off as though nothing had happened.

"It was nothing," Nitticello said. "Nothing at all. Just a touch of dizziness I suspect. Probably from driving in the storm. Back to your places, my Sashes. I'll summon you when I have further need of you."

Joe gulped. Heavy thunder was rolling over the valley, and if he had been alone he might have indulged in reflections of his own innocence. But just now, with the strange fire of Nitticello's eyes drilling him, he didn't even want to be innocent. He wanted to tear Nitticello to bits.

"Bathe and put on your clean slave rags," Nitticello said. "There's a basement room waiting for you. When you feel friendly, call for me. As I said before, I think we can do business."

CHAPTER SIX

SLAVE...Slave...are you there?"

"Pudge?" Joe peered into the darkness. He couldn't even see outlines of the stone walls in this basement room. He strained at his chains. They had taken no chance with him this time but had shackled him in irons.

"Sh-sh! Don't be rattling around. I'm coming."

Pudge's voice was close and intimate, as if he were right at Joe's ear. "What have they done? Bolted you down solid?"

"My ankles," Joe whispered. "They had a funny notion that I might walk out on them, I guess. But my hands are free. If you could bring me a file—"

"Not so fast, slave. Maybe I didn't come to release you."

"Oh, just a friendly visit? Now isn't that cozy?"

"Stop your growling, slave. Do you know what is going on around this place?"

"Plenty. After what I've seen this afternoon, you can't surprise me with anything."

"Oh, can't I?" There was mischief and intrigue in the frog-boy's voice. "I'll see about that. Stay right where you are till I get back."

"Where are you going?"

"There's a convention of frogs in the marsh." Pudge gave a weird little laugh.

"Stop it! Where are you going?"

"Past the King's window. Things are buzzing in his brain. Buzzing reminds me of flies and flies remind me of dinner—"

"Are you going to eavesdrop on the King?"

"Exactly. But I'll be back. Don't go away."

King Arvo Arvadello sat in his executive room, brooding. The rain had ceased. The deep darkness of night had come over the valley. He was alone.

He toyed with the heap of papers on his black marble desk. Troubles, troubles…it was an old story, he thought—a kingdom on the ragged edge of ruin; a young ruler who had no stomach for his job; and a crafty old adviser who was bleeding the kingdom for personal gain.

He glanced at the papers—riots. Three of the slave owners at

Redroot Hill had been murdered. The countryside was seething.

What had been done about it? Arvo shuffled the papers until he found Nitticello's report.

"Fifty more Sashes sent to Redroot Hill to restore order—Nitti."

Fifty Sashes. Would that throw a scare into a thousand rebellious slaves? Or just antagonize them?

A later report: "Seventeen slaves beaten near Redroot Hill. Ten reported dead." Yes, the Sashes had gone to work.

To this report Nitticello had pencilled a comment, "Excellent. This nips the rebellion in the bud. Redroot officers recommended for special honors—Nitti."

Nitti had the situation in hand, of course. Nitti was running things, when you came right down to it. And he was lining his own pockets in the process.

And yet King Arvo knew that without Nitti he would have been at a loss for the answers. Sooner or later he always turned to Nitti for help. Nitti was always there. He had always been there, for years prior to Arvo becoming King. That was the trouble.

"Why don't I call him in and tell him that from now on I'll make the decisions? Why do I keep postponing it?"

Impulsively, King Arvo touched a button. His personal attendant entered.

"Where is Nitticello at the moment?"

"He's out on the plaza, your majesty. He was asking whether you had approved his request for honors for the Redroot officers—"

"Do you have to bring that up? I'm busy." Arvo squirmed uneasily as he thought for a moment. He might just as well give Nitti his way on that point and get it over with. "All right, tell him to go ahead and grant the honors."

The King fancied he saw a look of pity in the attendant's eyes. Yes, the court must have observed. It was probably common gossip that he was always yielding.

"Do you wish me to turn on the lights?" the attendant asked.

"No, nothing more."

The attendant bowed and left.

It was pitch black beyond Arvo's open window. He stood there breathing in the moist night air slowly. Honors for the slave-beaters. Obstreperous slaves were killed the moment they became troublesome—that was Nitti's policy. There were plenty more to be had, as Nitti always said, and all kinds.

Arvo was presently haunted by thoughts of the Earth slave. His superb physique—almost a match for Arvo's own—and his face—something like Arvo's—and his rich pleasing voice, strong but restrained.

How did it feel, being a slave?

The question wedged into Arvo's consciousness too deeply for comfort.

"Stop sympathizing," he scolded himself. "He's only a miserable muddy slave...probably a criminal."

The King's thoughts were broken by the appearance of a

flaming torch, moving across the plaza…

WHEN Pudge returned to Joe's basement prison, he reported that the whole court had assembled out on the plaza for a religious observance. The nine torch lanterns had been lighted.

"If you listen you can hear them chanting. You've not heard anything until you've heard Karridonza music. It's even more soulful than a chorus of frogs." Pudge chortled. "You and I ought to be out there helping them."

"That's why I say. If you will get me a file—"

"But that isn't the real show, slave. It's just a screen. The real show is right down there." The frog boy took Joe's hand and touched it to the stone floor.

Joe mumbled something to indicate his confusion. For all he knew, Pudge may have been able to see through this stone floor. Those big ghastly green eyes of his—there was no telling what secret powers this curious creature possessed. But whatever the frog boy might mean, Joe was learning to have confidence in him.

"Give me a hand," Pudge was saying. "I've been in this cell before and I know which rock to work on. It's this one…it moves. It lifts—if you have what it takes."

Joe strained at his bonds and followed the boy's directions. The small stones that were wedged between the larger blocks of the floor presently loosened and came out. Then Joe applied his strength to the handle-like niches. The stone budged. Together they succeeded in lifting it and setting it to one side.

Joe looked down through the square into a deep, dimly lighted room below.

"Don't breathe," Pudge whispered. "They'll be here in a moment—Nitticello and the King. Listen…"

The source of the light that filtered into the cavernous room must have been moving, for little by little it revealed a series of curving white stone stairways constructed in a fantastic pattern. They formed what appeared to be an immense funnel directly

beneath Joe's gaze. Now Joe could see the King and the Prime
Minister as they jogged down these steps. The Prime Minister
was carrying a lantern. They descended one tier of stairs after
another, down and down, until they had reached a point about
one hundred feet beneath Joe's observation point.

The lantern was extinguished. But there was still a light—
one brilliant dot of purple, coming from the very center of that
deep funnel. It was a weird, far away glow coming from a point
so deep Joe thought it might have been the very center of the
earth.

"Listen," Pudge said. He took a small rock and tossed it. If
it had struck close, the two men would have heard it. But it fell
through the near darkness, straight down toward the deep well
of purple light.

Joe listened for several seconds. No sound returned.

"Deep," said Pudge. "Nobody knows how deep unless he
rides through on the vine."

Joe had heard many stories of the wonders and dangers of
this mysterious phenomenon. The lavender vine! Pudge
seemed to know all about it. The two men were about to call it
into action, he said. Joe's pulses quickened.

"What kind of a thing is it? Is it something that belongs to
the King?"

"It belongs to no one," Pudge said. "We belong to it, if
anything. It's as wild as the very lightning. No one knows when
it will come or what it will bring…or who'll get killed by it. And
not many people know where it sleeps. But I think this is its
home, right down there."

"Have you ever seen it?"

"Seen it? I was in it. I'm one of its victims. Did you think
that I was born with this monstrous form?"

The words made Joe to silence. He had seen so many
strange things in this land that he had taken Pudge for granted.
But Pudge's deepest feelings were betrayed by his low,
quavering voice. In this moment he had revealed the secret of
his life.

WITHIN the deep curve of the funnel, the King was pronouncing magic words. Joe could hear the mysterious mumbling in a language that was certainly not Karridonzan.

The dot of purple was rising. Like the bulb of a gigantic plant, it was sprouting into a stem. Now it emerged into the wider mouth of the funnel, a twisted trunk of purple light.

The brilliance was increasing. The King and the Prime Minister began to back away from it, keeping a close eye on it as they ascended a few steps. From deep purple it was changing into something brighter. Soon it was as luminous as an electric arc. A brilliant lavender.

It was a living thing, Joe thought.

It was extending into branches—the thick, limp arms of a sprangling vine. The arms were silky things of light. Whether they were flowing gases or solid substance Joe couldn't tell.

"Seevia...Seevia...Seevia."

The King had changed his chant into some sort of command. Pudge whispered to Joe that the word meant, "creep."

The vine was creeping, branching out into several directions over the walls of the funnel.

Several stems had ranged upward almost high enough to touch the underside of the floor through which they watched, so that Joe momentarily wondered what might happen if he, like Pudge, were caught within its power.

Pudge said, "Notice that the King has summoned it. But the Prime Minister will instruct it."

Joe saw that one branch near the central trunk was curved like the duct of a gigantic "ear" and into this "ear" the Prime Minister was speaking. He was giving instructions.

"Seevia...Seevia...Seevia..." the King's voice droned on ceaselessly.

Pudge swung down through the opening in the floor and before Joe could detain him, he leaped to the branch of the lavender light that was extending toward the ceiling.

Joe saw the vine bend and twist under the weight of the frog boy. It was like a roll of lavender-colored silk—smooth, flexible and yet with a certain living quality that made it sensitive to every touch.

The two men below did not see Pudge. The lad stole down as silent as the vine itself. Indeed, Joe was beginning to think of him as a part of this mysterious power. When he had reached the branching arm just above the "ear", he was careful not to be observed. The Prime Minister was working in earnest—at what, Joe could only guess.

Many minutes later the frog boy ascended to the ceiling. He had carried out his eavesdropping expedition successfully. By taking advantage of the bending and twisting of branches, he found his way back to the opening where Joe waited.

"Nitti is telling the vine to go to the wrecked air spinner." Pudge was excited over the news. "He tells it to bring back anything of great value that it finds there. See how the tips of the branches are waving. It's working. It's spreading long stems out across the valley. It finds its way through dozens of places. That room you see opens to the cliff beyond the palace. And there are caves straight down that also lead out."

"Can the people out in the valley see it?"

"If we were on top of the palace, we could see it streaming out in several directions."

"Can't you cut me loose from this anchor? I'd give my right arm for a view."

"If you want to sacrifice a leg," Pudge quipped, "we might chop you loose. But don't be impatient. The real show is here. Just wait. Wait till it brings back those jewels."

So this was the means that Nitticello had in mind when he assured the King that the treasures could be recovered.

"Nitticello was also telling it, 'No flesh...no bones,'" Pudge said.

That was the Prime Minister's concession to the King, Joe thought. The girl's crushed body was never to be seen. The King had simply vetoed that.

"Something's coming up the shaft," Pudge whispered. "You can tell by the way that main stem is trembling. It's coming—"

Up through the central trunk, an object was being conveyed. It rose like an immense leaf in a fountain—a light-colored rectangle of some material that Joe couldn't immediately identify—and it slid down through one of the branches and dropped with a thud at the Prime Minister's feet.

The Prime Minister and the King jumped back to avoid being struck. The thing had settled solidly, however, and they approached to examine it.

"Why, it's only the wing of the air spinner," Nitticello said audibly. "No, no. This won't do," he said loudly. "Bring what is valuable. Valuable!"

The King resumed his weird antics, gesturing and chanting. "Seevia…Seevia…Seevia…"

CHAPTER SEVEN

THE wing of the wrecked air spinner!

It had been sheared clean, like a knife blade. Joe seemed to feel it stab right through his body. The girl—the wreck! The two men were muttering. The Prime Minister was damning such outrageous luck; and the King, garbling his magic words, showed plainly enough his surprise that the lavender vine had apparently failed. But as Joe watched and listened, his only thought was of Marcia Melinda.

He whispered to Pudge. "If there's any way to get me out of this cell, I want to go—to her. On my planet we pay our respects to the dead. It's the least I can do—for her. Can you help me get loose?"

Pudge had an idea up his frog-skin sleeve. Again he lowered himself through the floor, holding tight to the edge with his hands. His shiny green legs kicked at the highest tongue of lavender light. His action apparently attracted it, for it waved higher. He kept teasing it as he crawled back to safety. The tip of silky lavender followed him through the opening. It snapped at him like a whip. He guided it across the floor to Joe's chains. It jumped and waved, as flexible as a rope of silk. Pudge brought it to Joe's ankles. Joe could feel warm air currents as it lashed toward him. A metallic *snap!* Then Joe's chains were chopped away clean. Joe, perspiring, rolled back out of reach. For a long moment he and Pudge huddled in the corner, watching. The lavender vine began to retreat, and presently it was gone.

Together Joe and Pudge replaced the stone in the floor. They made a quiet exit from the basement room. They ascended a dark stairway to the palace corridors.

"Side exit," Pudge advised.

With chanting going on in the front and the lavender vine cutting an errant path from the rear, there wasn't much choice. The corridors of the palace were completely empty, fortunately. No guard remained at his post during the torch lantern services.

They reached the side porch; they quietly ascended to the balcony for a better view of the valley.

The lighted lavender path lay in a curious zigzag pattern over hillsides and through groves of trees. As Pudge remarked, it looked like a fifty mile bolt of lightning that had frozen and fallen across the ground.

"At the farther end of the lavender vine I'll find the body of the American girl," Joe said. "I'm going at once."

"You'd better set your stakes for a long hike, slave. It will take you all night and half of tomorrow."

"Aren't you coming with me?"

The frog boy might not have heard. The chanting voices from the plaza caused him to edge along in that direction for a view of the torch ritual. He sighed. Certain deep emotions had been stirred in him, Joe thought. For all his froggish appearance there was something very human about him.

They were putting out the torches now, extinguishing one after each stanza of their melancholy song. Joe saw that Pudge was being drawn into the ritual as if by magic. He had begun to sing to himself, and his bright green eyes were shining intently.

He climbed down over a trellis, hopped through a fountain, moved quietly into the red light of the last torch and sat there swaying to the music. He ducked back into the fountain when they came too close, but he was a part of the ritual now, and it wouldn't let him go.

"So long, Pudge," Joe said under his breath.

Left to his own devices, Joe waited for a flare of faraway lightning that would reveal a few landmarks. It wasn't going to be easy, spotting the point where the lavender vine ended.

An hour later he was hiking through the darkness. A few lights through the valley were constant enough to give him his direction.

A few hours later a pink dawn broke through a striped sky. Horizontal lines of hard blue clouds framed the red sun as it rose above the dark mists of the horizon. Sometime in the night the storm had rolled away. And the mysterious river of lavender light across the valley had folded back into itself and melted away in the blackness.

Morning brought news of five deaths in the valley. The trail of the vine was always marked with tragedy. Terror spread as rapidly as the rumors could fly. The lavender vine! Why had it come again? Where did it come from? Was there any reason that it should choose a trail through the lowlands? Had it chosen its victims with a hand to justice? No one knew.

Every group of peasants or slaves that Joe passed was buzzing with excited talk. Every person felt that he might have been one of the victims. It was hungry lightning on the loose. Well, five victims should satisfy its appetite for awhile.

It was going to be easier than Joe had feared, following the trail to the wrecked plane. Every wisp of conversation he overheard guided him. Occasionally other slaves tried to stop him for questions, when their masters weren't close by. He kept hiking, like a good slave on a cross-country errand. For the most part he was able to slip past the masters and the peasants. At the edge of one village he was tempted to stop and talk with a peasant woman who had paused to admire her pretty face in the brook—or was she only adjusting the blue scarf on her head?

Joe resisted the impulse, however. She hadn't seen him. He slipped around the village unnoticed and hurried on his way.

Late that afternoon he came to the end of the trail. The crumpled metal of a wrecked air spinner lay scattered across the hillside. Apparently the wreck had not been discovered. It had occurred within the screen of rain and no one had seen it happen. The muddy rain that had gathered on the pieces after the fall showed no signs of having been touched by human hands.

Where was the body of the girl?

Joe searched the hillside until nightfall. It was a vain search. He couldn't understand it. There was no sign of a victim.

Darkness came over him. Tomorrow he would search farther. Exhausted, he fell asleep on the ground.

He was awakened by his own fitful dreams. He was weak and hungry. Perhaps there was food to be found somewhere in the wreckage. He staggered back and began to putter around in the darkness.

Far away he could see a row of lights that must have been the palace Reddish lights. He counted nine.

"The religious ritual," he said aloud. "I wonder if Pudge is singing with them."

Having spoken aloud, he stopped to wonder whether anyone might have heard. Several times he had been pleasantly surprised by the unexpected appearance of Pudge just when he needed company.

"Pudge!" he called. "Pudge!"

There was no answer. The dark valley was all his own. Nothing but black outlines of hills against the dark mists that bordered the starry sky. A few distant lights—villages or lonely farm homes—and a twisting lavender stream of light...

The lavender vine!

It was creeping along the valley like a narrow ribbon of

luminous silk over a landscape of black velvet.

It was coming toward him. Its nearest branch not less than five miles away, and moving rapidly. It was coming toward the air spinner again, of course. It would try again tonight to recover the treasure of gems.

"Pudge!" Joe's voice sounded tight and scared.

It was coming fast, weaving around the groves of trees, skipping over the tops of rocks. Joe froze in his tracks for a moment fascinated.

A village lay in its path. Strangely, it lifted over the top, like an arched bridge, then struck the ground and skipped, like the path of a skipping stone.

Joe was backing away from the wreckage now. He was suddenly running. It was less than a mile away and many miles of it were visible. Joe thought of the terrorized people who must be awakening all along the valley from the flare of lavender light in their windows. What persons would be caught within its deadly grip tonight?

The peasant woman? The woman who had stopped to adjust her scarf in the mirror of the brook. Joe couldn't help thinking of her, wondering—

He stumbled and fell. He scrambled to his feet and raced on around the slope. He needed to get well out of range. The vine was coming toward the wreckage by the swiftest possible course. He could see the tip end now. That was the "growth bud", he thought. It was less than two hundred yards from him. What a fascinating thing. He slackened his retreat long enough to observe its weird form. The growing end was branched like the delta of a river—or like a bolt of lightning that reaches with a cluster of fingers. The fingers lifted over trees and rocks, touched the ground, and lifted again. Where the fingers went the long twisting zigzag arm followed.

A claw of light, Joe thought. No head or face or eyes, but a claw, like a living thing, feeling its way forward, racing over the land in search of something—something Joe was certain were the lost jewels of King Arvo and Prime Minister Nitticello.

Now it came to the wreckage. The lavender fingers played over the fragments. Nothing moved from the ground. Light glinted from pieces of metal and glass. But nothing lifted. It was like some monster musician running his electric fingers over a mute instrument. Nothing moved. Nothing sounded.

Joe was hypnotized by the sight. He wanted to creep closer. If only he knew what Pudge knew about controlling this runaway power.

The lavender vine gave a surprise leap away from the wreckage. Its fingers struck the hillside twice, elongating, jumped furiously through the blackness. They leaped at Joe and caught him. For an instant he felt the tingle of something mildly warm and electrical pulsating through his body. Then the pressure of the lavender claw tightened. A whirl of colored images blinded him and then everything was black and he was devoid of feeling.

CHAPTER EIGHT

ON the same morning that Joe had watched the red sun rise through the striped clouds, an American girl had walked through the same Karridonzan Valley, wondering what the new day would bring forth. Marcia Melinda knelt over a pool of water and studied her reflection carefully. There wasn't much more she could do to disguise herself as a peasant woman. She simply wasn't going to cut her hair Karridonza fashion. No one would know as long as she wore the dark blue scarf.

A few low white clouds scuffed away into the purple mists beyond the valley. The bright light of day was her enemy today. She mustn't let her identity be discovered. And yet she must get to a village somewhere. Her plight was a desperate one. Here she was, an American diplomat, wandering across an alien world with a satchel of priceless royal jewels in her possession. Marcia knew she needed to convert the jewels into money—and soon. But by what methods, and to whom? Somewhere she hoped to find the right person.

As she walked along she also considered her options for

using the money. She knew there was no returning to Earth at this point. She knew the Prime Minister's men would come searching for the crashed air spinner. When her body and the jewels were not found inside the wreckage, all the Sashes in the kingdom would be sent out to capture her. Even if she was able to sell the jewels, there was slim chance of her legally boarding an Earthbound rocket at the skystation. The Prime Minister's men would most certainly be watching. Her only option left was to somehow use the money against the King and the Prime Minister. As a diplomat sent from Earth to discuss the very issue of slavery, she was very aware of slave and rebel unrest among the citizens. Rumors of a brewing rebellion had been circulating for several years. Perhaps she could funnel the money into the hands of an organized rebel group. She wondered, though—would the anxiety of her plight show in her countenance? Would it give her away? She must avoid meeting too many people.

What a stormy night it had been—not one storm but several. That terrifying ride in the air spinner would certainly have been fatal, however, if it hadn't been for the rain. The rain had obscured her from view as soon as she had taken to the air, and she was able to parachute down almost at once, unseen by the watchers at the palace.

As if she hadn't known what Nitticello was up to when all of those elaborate gifts came forth. Making her sign that friendship document—the murder in his eyes had shown too clearly. Her fear had been that the American slave would be allowed to accompany her, and that would have certainly spelled death for him. It had been a last second attempt at reverse psychology when she urged the Prime Minister to let him come along instead of declining his service as pilot—and it had worked.

"The American—I wonder what he's like," she wondered aloud.

She was somewhat surprised to realize how much interest she had taken in him at first sight. Her kiss to him had originally been a dodge—anything to avoid that arrogant guard. But the tall, well-built American had looked at her so imploringly—and then so gratefully.

She wondered whether he, as an American, was as mystified over Karridonzan ways as she. Had he seen the weird vein of light that crawled through the valley last night? It must have been the lavender vine, the lavender vine that so many people had spoke of in hushed tones. She had heard legends of the many deaths it had wrought. She had been less than a mile away from the wrecked air spinner when it had suddenly appeared—it was one danger she hadn't foreseen.

She couldn't help wondering—did someone at the palace hold some kind of control over that phenomenon? After all, it had come from the palace's general direction. Perhaps it had been sent to overtake her. She glanced at the cloth bag that hung innocently from her arm, then quickened her step.

"They'll soon discover that my body isn't anywhere in the wreckage," she thought aloud. "And all the riches they lavished upon me will have vanished."

When that was discovered, Marcia knew her life wouldn't be worth the smallest pearl in her newfound collection.

Before high noon she had talked with slaves in three different fields along the way. She had tried to probe them about their feelings regarding their enslavement. Had they any thoughts or plans of fighting for their freedom?

Their answers and reactions had been quite guarded. Some had stared at her in obvious suspicion. Was she a member of some counter-intelligence group sent from the palace? Or was she a genuine slave sympathizer who might be a member of one the various slave groups? Did she know the details of what had happened to the slaves at Redroot Hill?

"Please believe me," she would reply. "Please believe that I want to help all of the slaves in the kingdom. I know the location of some priceless items—items that can be sold for a great deal of money—possibly enough to help fund a movement that could bring an end to slavery."

The slaves were still suspicious, though. However, one particularly rugged-looking individual mentioned—offhand—that he might allow her to attend a secret meeting where she could explain more fully her plans for helping them. She would have to contact him later, though—after she sold her items.

"As to your priceless items," he told her, "if you want to dispose of them you should take them to the merchant, Nadoff, when you reach the village." Other slaves along the way had also agreed that Nadoff was the one man who could help her.

HER feet were aching, and she was hungry and weary long before she reached the village. She was put to the limits of her ingenuity, dodging the slave masters and travelers along the way, or inventing excuses for her passing conversations with the slaves. At one village she concocted a story that she was traveling through the region looking for her lost son who had been sold into slavery.

"Your son?" the local slave master asked skeptically. He frowned and remarked that she certainly wasn't old enough to be the mother of a grown son. In fact, he doubted from her accent that she was even a native Karridonzan. "But you're a pretty enough little thing," he commented with a salacious twinkle in his eye. "And if you're a stray wandering about homeless...I can certainly find a shelter for you."

She hurried on, though, drawing her blue scarf tight around her throat. The slave master's comments hung in her mind. She did look too young. Outside the village she stopped at a brook and did her best to darken the rings under her eyes and add years to her face using the little makeup she had in her possession.

Late that afternoon Marcia came to the village where Nadoff lived. She found him to be a round, jolly merchant who could laugh loud enough to make the vases on his shelves quiver. He gave her the heartiest of receptions. After exchanging pleasantries she took him aside. Nadoff motioned her toward a corner table where they both sat down.

"I have something quite private I wish to discuss," she said. "I have some valuable jewels in my possession—the finest I have ever seen."

Nadoff swallowed hard and then burst into an uproar of laughter. "You're joking. What fine jewels could you possibly have?"

"Have you heard of the Earth girl who was recently visiting the King?"

"Yes I have," the merchant answered, "but there have been rumors of her death—most recently in fact."

"She's not dead. *I* am that girl. My name is Marcia Melinda. I've been here on a diplomatic mission. Yesterday I was scheduled to return to Earth. When I started to leave the palace, the King and the Prime Minister gave me some gifts of jewels, a considerable number of them—and they are *quite* valuable."

Marcia pulled the bag of jewels out and placed it on the table in front of Nadoff.

"Then they tried to murder me."

Nadoff's jolly disposition suddenly vanished. Marcia looked at him earnestly and continued in a low voice.

"I'd like to use these jewels to help your oppressed people…the slaves. I'm sure they're worth a small fortune. I have no way at this point of legally getting back to my home planet. I'd be taken prisoner at any spaceport." A reflective look came over her face. "And if I know Prime Minister Nitticello, I'm sure I'd meet a quick death. All I can do is try to help the people of this oppressed world. I was originally sent here from Earth to scrutinize slave conditions on this planet." She chuckled slightly under her breath. "But it's gotten me far more than I bargained for. So at this point it seems I'm forced to move from diplomacy to…insurrection."

Nadoff's expression had become quite serious. It quickly became obvious that the secret movement of the slaves was close to his heart. However his face darkened with a look of disbelief. He was prepared to ask Marcia many questions, but when she opened the bag and he caught sight of the extraordinary cache of jewels in her possession, he was—for the moment—stunned to silence. He arose and motioned her to follow him. A moment later he was leading her into a back room where they again sat at a table to talk.

"Now we can speak more freely," he said. There was a grave expression on his face. "Now tell me everything. Right from the beginning—"

It wasn't easy for Marcia to cut away the curtains of suspicion. After she had talked with Nadoff for nearly an hour, relating her experiences at the palace, the merchant called in two of his compatriots. Marcia was soon retelling her story to the two of them.

"So you see, the jewels are mine," she concluded. "It's true that I wasn't meant to live long after receiving them, but they are mine nonetheless." She looked directly into Nadoff's eyes. "I am trusting you…a total stranger…with my life. Is it too much risk for you to try to sell them, and use the money as I have suggested?"

The three men said nothing. Finally Nadoff arose and said, "wait here."

He and the other two men left the room and considered Marcia's story for several minutes. Presently Nadoff reappeared and said, "Tonight there will be a secret meeting not far from here. We would like you to attend. However, I must warn you, we never know when we may be discovered by the Sashes, but you seem to be sincere—"

"I'll be honored to attend," Marica cut in.

CHAPTER NINE

NITTICELLO couldn't get an answer out of the frog boy. He spent the afternoon trying various tortures on the lad—a pleasant way to pass the hours, if one is versed in the arts of inflicting pains upon others. To Nitticello, pleasure was pleasure, and the more he could make some guilty soul shriek, the more he enjoyed himself.

The frog boy had been discovered on the previous night during the latter part of the torch lantern ceremony. One of the Sashes had remembered Pudge. A nuisance, a little misshapen vagabond who was always getting himself under foot at the gates of the fortress. He had been told many times before to stay away. And here he was, participating in one of the religious rituals as proudly as if he might have been a second cousin to the King.

Whips apparently had little effect upon Pudge, the Prime Minister had observed. And the application of hot irons always caused the elusive little fellow to leap out of reach, even though he had been chained. Chains didn't hold Pudge. He was a slippery, amorphous creature and one could no more bind him than nail down a shadow. But when cornered, he would scream with pain, whether he was being touched or not, and although Nitticello couldn't be sure that the pain was real, the effect was satisfying. However, Nitticello's question about the American slave brought no answer from Pudge. And in this regard, the ordeal was a failure.

"I've tried everything," the Prime Minister told the King that evening. "I don't believe that wretched frog child knows the answer. The slave has gotten away without leaving a trace."

The King was about to suggest a course of action. As usual, the Prime Minister beat him to it.

"I suggest, Arvo, that we dispatch some Sashes to scour the country. He can't have gone far on foot. He should be brought back—"

"Or should he be returned to his master?" the King offered, as if debating his own decision rather than sounding out his adviser.

"He should be brought here," the Prime Minister said decisively. "The law on that point is clear."

The King said no more. He led the way to the basement cavern. Again the night's chanting had commenced around the lanterns on the plaza. That was the best time to invite the lavender vine—when the rest of the court wouldn't know. Tonight it was Nitti's purpose to complete the unfinished business of recovering the jewels.

King Arvo had come to a turning point. The mental agony of being dominated by this little wrinkled old sadist must be brought to an end. Tonight Arvo would begin. The first matter that came up for a decision would be the starting point. He would make his own decision, and he would force it down Nitti's throat.

Perhaps the drastic action Nitticello had taken against the American girl had brought Arvo's dilemma to a crisis. He had spent a sleepless night of remorse—remorse and resolution, remorse for his own indecisiveness, resolution to break the domination.

Yes, King Arvo was going to rule. And Nitticello was going to obey—or lose his position as Prime Minister.

The bluish-white light from the lantern illuminated the cavern beneath the palace. The two men crossed to their usual station. Nitticello was being pessimistic. He doubted whether the King could invoke the lavender vine two nights in succession. Arvo said to himself, "He's challenging me. My powers over the vine are still a mystery to him."

The light was extinguished. All of the King's pent up feelings gave weight to his voice as he went through the hoarsely whispered, "Seevia…Seevia…Seevia."

He felt a glow of triumph, then, when the trunk of the pinkish blue light began to form out of the blackness, he moved back. Swiftly the strands of silken lavender reached their arms out over the cliff and down into the valley. Nitticello would see. From this hour forward Arvo would prove himself a tower of strength. He flexed his muscles. He thought of the similarly fine physique of the American slave. Power, confidence stubborn determination. Those were the qualities that belonged with a sturdy build and powerful muscles.

NOW Nitticello was trying his powers. He was calling for

action. The valuables, the treasure—it would be found near the wrecked spinner. Or in the pocket of some thief who had passed that way. It should be recovered. It should be delivered to this step. Over and over he pronounced his demands.

At last the sprangling branches of the vine began to vibrate. Something was coming.

Arvo stood his ground. Would it be the jewels this time? Was Nitticello's own special demand being answered at last? If so, which of them would reach to pick up the treasure when it fell at their feet?

The lavender vine shook with a mighty wave and deposited its treasure—a man.

The fellow dropped limply at King Arvo's feet and lay there not moving.

"The slave...the Earth fellow..."

That was all King Arvo could say at the moment. Nitticello stared, moved a step closer, and touched his sandal to the slave's head. The prostrated fellow showed signs of life. The shock of being carried over the miles through the vine had stunned him. His eyes were half-open, his lips began to mumble something unintelligible, and his breathing was heavy.

Nitti scowled. "We call for a treasure and we get this. We've missed it again."

"Another disappointment," Arvo said.

"Were you wishing for him instead of the gems?" Nitti asked, and the tone of accusation was in his voice. "Very well, this isn't the worst possible luck."

"What do you mean?" the King asked, for he had sensed that Nitti foresaw some special use for this prisoner.

"I mean—nothing. I was afraid he was gone."

"He'll be gone tomorrow," the King said.

"Gone, where?"

"I'm condemning him to death."

The slave's eyes opened wider. He must have caught the idea. He looked around, evidently realizing that he had returned to his captors.

"Don't do anything rash, Arvo," Nitticello suggested casually. "I think we may find him useful."

King Arvo's jaw tightened. Here it was—the test. Nitticello

was trying to take the situation out of his hands.

"The law is plain," King Arvo said, meeting Nitticello's eye. "As the ruler of this kingdom, I hereby condemn this slave to die tomorrow."

Nitticello came back with a quick word of warning. "You'd better keep your eye on him, then. He's vicious. Don't forget that he broke out of irons once. And here we stand unguarded."

Nitticello began to back away. The King was left to visualize what might happen if the prone man should suddenly spring to his feet. It was Arvo's impulse to retreat. But once again he stood solid. And then, as the slave came up on his elbows, Arvo surprised himself by striking the fellow.

One quick blow to the jaw—that was enough.

The slave sank back to the ground and closed his eyes, and he looked to be a very sick man.

King Arvo drew a deep breath of strength. He knew he had surprised Nitticello. He knew that Nitti was eyeing him wondering what had come over him. But King Arvo simply folded his arms and said, "I'll stand by, Nitti, until you send in a pair of Sashes."

CHAPTER TEN

JOE was almost too sick to know or care what was going on. He doubted whether even Pudge would be optimistic under these conditions. His hands were bound behind him, his ankles were fastened securely, and he was imprisoned within a cell of steel bars.

Across the way, Nitticello and Stobber were talking earnestly.

"I've known all along this would come...sooner or later," Nitticello said. "Last night it happened. The King has done it. He's stepped out from under us. Unless we take desperate measures, this may spell the end for us."

That was all Joe heard before lapsing into a sleep of exhaustion.

Stobber and Nitticello had exchanged guarded confidences before. At times of crisis they knew how to understand and work with each other. Nitti was freely admitting that he had never before felt such a feeling of urgency regarding his relationship with the King.

"You'll think of something," Stobber said giving him a wink of confidence.

"I've thought of it already," the Prime Minister responded. He put his hand on Stobber's shoulder. "It's a two-man job. And there's only one person in the world I would dare trust with this situation, and that's you. Believe me my friend, there will be rewards aplenty for you when we succeed."

"Go ahead—I'm listening."

"We've got to act fast. The King is determined to execute this man. We have less than two hours."

"It's air tight," Stobber growled. "If you've got any notion of saving him, that's out. We've already announced the assembly of officers. They are already gathering, waiting for the King to march up and read the death sentence."

"That's why we've got to act quickly. Time is of the essence. Haven't you noticed the resemblance?"

"What resemblance?"

"The slave and the king...they look identical. They could be twin brothers."

"Hard to see anything through all that filth and unkempt hair."

"True," Nitticello responded, "but I've had a good look at him up close—a very good look. This slave and the King look so much alike that if you gave them both a clean shave and rolled them in a barrel, you wouldn't be able to tell which one was which." A malevolent smile crept across the Prime Minister's face. "Now don't you see the beauty of it my dear Stobber—it's so obvious what we must now do."

"You mean?"

"Yes...yes we must make them trade places."

Even Stobber, a malicious individual at best, was a taken

aback by this, but the Prime Minster pressed on.

"Think of it," Nitti continued, "the King will be executed by the King's own orders. It couldn't be more perfect."

Stobber gave an uneasy groan. He had great anxiety about their chances of success. What about the slave's voice? His mannerisms? His ability to perform even the least demanding of the King's duties? How could they be sure that he would behave in the manner they demanded of him, and in the manner befitting of a king?

But Nitticello was determined, and frankly tired of wet-nursing a weak young royal who—in Nitticello's mind at least—had no business sitting on the throne. The delicate game of control he played with the King had reached the brink. If King Arvo burst into a new invigorated feeling of self-confidence, then Nitti's special shelf of luxuries and power would be put into jeopardy.

"You'll need to get a shaving outfit, Stobber. Get one of the King's court suits, too. And don't let anyone see you."

Stobber finally agreed—reluctantly. They went over the fine details of the plot for several minutes.

It's time," Nitticello finally said. "I'll get the King."

Five minutes later King Arvo and the Prime Minister walked up to the cell.

Joe was rousing out of his sleep. A low conversation penetrated his consciousness. The King and Nitti. Nitti was talking nervously. Without opening his eyes Joe listened.

"I tell you, Arvo, you've got to talk with him. I think he knows what happened to the girl. It stands to reason. The vine itself pulled him back to us from the wrecked spinner. That *must* mean he had some connection with her. Maybe he has hidden the jewels himself."

King Arvo shook his head. "The fellow's half dead. Can't you give him something to wake him up, at least long enough for his execution?"

"Execution—oh, yes..." Nitti appeared to have forgotten this detail. "But after he's gone, we'll never find out—don't you see—we've got to drag this secret out of him first."

They opened the door of the cell and entered. Nitticello produced a hypodermic needle. "Here's something that ought to loosen his tongue."

Joe was thoroughly awake now. The needle jabbed his arm. He was helpless to resist, but he couldn't help wondering what Nitticello had in mind. Nitticello the schemer.

Then Joe looked at the King pityingly, realizing that the poor fellow had been hounded into this situation—this mad determination to have his own way for once.

"Look out!" Joe yelled. Too late he had seen the shadow of Stobber. The husky chief of the Sashes strode in like a cyclone and struck the King across the back of the head before anyone could know what was coming.

The King's knees sagged and he fell. Nitticello had another needle for him. Then the two men went to work, one of them on the King and the other on Joe.

TEN minutes later they had effected a transformation that was nothing short of miraculous in Joe's opinion. He saw himself in the mirror that they held before him and he could hardly believe it. He was King Arvo Arvadello, yes, in every detail of appearance except for one thing. They had wrapped a white cloth around his throat. "Remember, King," Stobber was saying sarcastically, "you've got an awful bad cold. You can't talk well. Isn't that right, Nitti?"

"Yes, such a bad cold," said Nitti, "that he can't say anything except what I tell him to say."

Joe didn't fail to get the idea. He scrutinized the trim drooping mustache, the small spade-shaped back beard, the richly ornamented blue coat with the gold epaulets, and he knew that the court would accept him.

Then he turned his eyes upon the sorry figure that lay on the floor, garbed in slave's clothes. So that was Arvo—no, it was the Karridonzan version of Joe Peterson.

"He's too white," Nitti was saying, looking at the drugged

king. "And he's almost too heavy with sleep. We've got to make sure he's somewhat awake, at least long enough to go through with his own death sentence."

Stobber gave an evil laugh. "That's irony for you. He got stubborn and insisted on forcing his will upon us, didn't he?

They bronzed the King's face, chest, and extremities with lotions until he looked as if he had gone through a season of work under the sun. They had trouble enough with his hair, making fast the dabs of hair that they had shorn from Joe's head. Joe, observing, felt a loss of earthly pride to be wearing a make believe Karridonzan mane over his freshly shaved head.

One last detail they could not overlook. They gave their new slave the markings of a black eye—a match for the discoloration

which Arvo's fist had bestowed upon Joe's face the night before. Then they slapped Arvo on the cheeks.

"Anything to say before we gag you?"

"He can't talk," said Stobber. "He's too knocked out for it."

But Nitticello took no chances. He fixed a stout gag between Arvo's teeth and bound it with a bandage around his head. Bound hand and foot, the King was carried out of the cell and down the corridor to face his own order for execution.

"All right, your majesty," Nitticello said, turning to Joe. "This is your chance to perform. No slips. I have two extra needles and I'll be right beside you every minute. Do you understand what I'm doing for you?"

"You've saving my life," Joe said.

"Good. I think we understand each other."

CHAPTER ELEVEN

WORD of the execution had spread quickly and crowds were gathering at the execution grounds. Although their notice had been short, they promenaded down the sulfur-colored walk, dressed in their starchiest holiday clothes. Executions were, oddly enough, a dress-up occasion. For miles around, work had been suspended so that peasants and slave-masters alike could attend. They came from all directions—public-spirited Karridonzans, their manes of hair roached high in keeping with the importance of the event.

The chief topic of gossip, however, was not the execution. Most of the people, whether from the court or from the surrounding region, knew very little about the Earth-born slave who was to lose his life. That was nothing to them.

The important thing which made their conversations buzz was the return of the lavender vine.

It had come two nights in succession. The old timers were shaking their heads over the deadly toll it had taken. Twelve more on the second visit. Seventeen persons left dead in its path. Two nights of terror.

What would be done about it? Would the King make any mention of it at today's assembly? Had he any power in dealing with it? Did he realize that many citizens throughout the kingdom believed that the vine had come from the palace itself?

"The King should make some statement," people were saying. Or, "Perhaps we can gain a hearing with the Prime Minister." Or, "We're going to camp right here on the steps of the palace, my family and I, until we know the valley is safe again."

And there were more anguished reports that reached Nitti's ears: "Did you hear about our neighbor's little boy? It struck him in his sleep...seeped right in through the open window, bounded through his body and on through the wall..." "...We lost three cattle and a slave. Tomorrow we meant to take them all to the market..."

Nitticello listened, and the chills of uncertainty tingled through his spine. The lavender vine had always troubled him. It had put those tight wrinkles in his face—worry lines. His sleepless nights had never been caused by a conscience full of remorse for his acts of cruelty; they had come from trying to devise a way of achieving mastery over the lavender vine. It had troubled him, even possessed him, mentally, for many years. He had never let King Arvo know it, but in his twisted, control-driven mind the strange lavender entity had beaten him over and over again. After all these years, he had never learned the skill of calling it into his service the way others had in the past.

And yet the King possessed this skill.

Well, the King would soon be out of the way, and Nitti would have everything his own way. Yes, as long as he could keep a whip hand over the young American impostor...and as long as no one but Stobber ever knew the fate of the real king.

At the execution grounds a short while later, an important townsman confronted Nitticello with an earnest plea.

"Nitticello, you must make the King do something about the lavender vine."

"I'm busy now—"

The Prime Minister waved him off, but the townsman persisted.

"See that I have a chance to talk with the King right after the execution. Will you do that?"

141

"I'll do my best."

NITTI hurried away, mopping the perspiration from his forehead. He shook off requests and demands, right and left. His own complicated piece of engineering must be taken care of before he dared think of anything else.

But at least their obsession with the creeping lavender death had lightened their interest in the execution. In a few minutes it would be over, forgotten. Just one more unruly slave checked off, they would think. And Nitti's path would be clear.

The officers were seating themselves to the left and the right of the execution apparatus—two banks of seats like a small stadium. Seating capacity for not more than several hundred persons. The peasants and some of the townsmen would have to crowd against the fences for their share of the view. Several hundred persons of importance: officers of the court, slave owners, a few interplanetary tradesmen, Captains of the Sashes, etc.

Wealth, Nitti thought, as he glanced over the crowd. The private treasures of gems and precious metals—if they could be squeezed into his own hands—would be enough to buy the Karridonzan skystation and add in to the valley kingdom. And what a monopoly that would be—what a beautiful funnel for more riches from the passing trade between planets. Nitti's eyes rested on the sulfur-yellow walk, now almost cleared of the hurrying throngs, and for the moment he was seeing a shower of gold before his eyes.

The Sashes took their places in a double line, waiting for the condemned slave to be marched out to the bench. The "King," resplendent in his blue uniform, but apparently troubled by a sore throat, had been waiting in his private station in the center of the execution grounds. Now Nitti marched to this station, ascended the steps, and officially presented the "King."

"Rise and bow," Nitti whispered. The American in the guise of the King rose with dignity, hesitated as if not certain whether he was well enough to be standing on his two feet, then bowed in a satisfactory manner. The crowd rose and saluted him. He returned the salute. The crowd cheered, and he might have returned the cheer, but Nitti touched his arm…

"Enough, enough. Sit down. I'll give you your cues."

Stobber pranced in, followed by a quartet of Sashes surrounding the condemned man. The real king would never have been mistaken for anything but a badly beaten slave. Four ropes, wrapped around his half-clad body, led to the four Sashes conducting him; each one of them had a secure hitch on him. He was still gagged so that he couldn't utter a word; but no one would have heard him anyway, for now the crowd was getting keyed up and into the spirit of the affair. Everyone shouted, and the clamor went on until the condemned man had seated himself on the bench…

JOE Peterson swallowed hard and touched his throat. The wrappings were uncomfortable, and he tried to recall why he must pretend he had a sore throat. The afternoon sun blazed off the yellowish pavement of the execution grounds and burned at his eyes. He was sick. They had drugged him. They had done it so he would cooperate. Yes, he was supposed to yield to Nitticello's every suggestion—that was the price he was paying to save his own life.

Oh, yes, he was the King. That was it. He—Joe Peterson—was the King! Of course…that's what he had to keep in mind. He was supposed to run the entire affair because everybody thought he was the King and that's what they expected him to do.

And why was he putting on such a show? To execute the real king, of course.

Joe shook his head dizzily. Execute him, why?

"What are we doing this for?" Joe whispered to Nitti.

"Quiet. I'll explain later. Just do as I say."

"But we're about to kill the real king—hell, we don't want to do that. Do we?"

"Shut up—your *majesty*."

Joe gulped. The time had come. Joe looked down at the apparatus. It was black and shiny—rather pretty, in fact. Worm gears and little gun-like muzzles and lots of electrical apparatus, and also a long jointed blue bar of metal that led right up to the station where he was sitting. It had a red handle. Joe wore a white glove. He wondered if any of the red would come off on the glove.

Nitti had explained something about all that equipment a little while ago. Now Joe tried to recall what he had said. The use of the ray gun principle—that was it. The rays would slice in vertically, acting on a double-spiral control that caused them to move in from each side, like two vertical walls closing in. Only these walls would be invisible, and they would disintegrate whatever they touched.

Disintegrate—that was what Nitti had said. A rather nasty word, disintegrate. It meant that the victim's body would start melting away from each side, as if it were being sliced away by a knife on each side. *Slice…slice…slice.* Both sides at once. Shoulders and arms first. Longitudinal sections from the shoulders to the elbows. And gradually the ears, a little at a time, and the jaws…

This was going to be interesting to watch, Joe thought. Only why? Had Nitti explained that, too? Joe asked again, or started to.

"Why did you say about—"

"Shut up."

Anyway it was an ingenious machine. It would give both sides of the stadium an equal view of the show all the time, until the very last cross-section of the victim was sliced away.

The time had come. Joe felt the nudge from Nitti. He reached for the lever. This wasn't right, he thought. But who was he to change the rules?

His hand was limp. He was almost too weak to reach.

"Read the sentence first," Nitti was saying, nudging him again.

"Oh…sure. The sentence." he took the paper from Nitti's

hand, an edged up to the microphone. He couldn't read a word of the writing, but Nitti had helped him to practice the speech, and now Nitti prompted him with whispers.

"I, Arvo Arvadello, King of the Karridonzan Valley," Joe began, "do hereby administer the punishment of death to this slave—"

Slave—yes, of course—this should have been for him, only they had switched the costumes.

"—for the high offense of breaking his bonds and escaping from the court prison. May the gods of Karridonza—"

What gods? Would the gods approve a turnabout like this, letting a king die for a slave?

"—witness the justice of my act."

Joe put down the paper, thinking to himself, so this is how it feels to be a king?

THEN his white-gloved hand went to his side, so tight that it was going to take an awfully tough nudge from Nitti this time. It was worse because the eyes of the real king were on him. The real king had been drugged too, Joe thought; but he knew what was happening. And he was looking up with the very same expression Joe would have had if he himself had been down there, about to be sliced away into nothing.

"Reach for the handle," Nitti whispered.

A sort of breathy *o-o-o-oh* went over the crowd as Joe reached. The gasp seemed to come from all the way back to the crowds at the fence. This was the moment.

"Pull the lever."

Joe shook his head. His drugged mental haze was beginning to lift. There must be some way out of this hellish task. He then caught sight of a well-dressed figure approaching the execution stand.

"There's someone else coming. I'll wait a moment."

"The lever—"

"It's an officer," Joe said. "I'll wait till he comes closer."

The microphone caught Joe's words. The crowd turned, and

the throngs around the yellow walk made way for a high Karridonzan officer who was coming in tardily.

"You're late, my friend," Joe shouted into the microphone. Nitti tried to hush him.

The officer called back, saluting, "I am late for a good reason, your majesty."

"Then come up here and tell me about it," Joe yelled.

The officer could hardly believe what he was hearing.

"Now, your majesty?"

"Now."

"But your majesty…" the officer implored, "…the execution…"

"*Now.*"

Though Nitti was exasperated, there was little he could do, for a royal command was a royal command. The officer came up, bubbling over with enthusiasm and embarrassment at the same time. The crowd was confused over the sudden change of events. A few of them even booed, but more were simply hushed, trying to hear the exchange between the officer and the King.

"Well, your majesty, I've just concluded the most wonderful business for you and the kingdom," he said, smiling. "As your faithful treasury agent—authorized to make purchases with royal funds—I have just purchased a wealth of new gems for your treasury. They are some of the most precious stones I have ever encountered, each fully examined and authenticated by a local gemologist. Look and see…"

The agent opened a beautiful silk and leather purse and revealed to Joe and Nitti the good fortune that was theirs. Joe's eyes widened at the sight. Pearls, rubies, emeralds. Necklaces and tiaras and bracelets and rings—

Nitti gave a gulp that might have choked the microphone.

"You—you bought them?" the Prime Minister stammered.

"From one of the village merchants. An interesting story— some peasant lady had offered them for sale."

"You've *paid* for them?" Nitti was becoming very red in the face.

"We did indeed have to pay a very large sum. However, the gemologist assured me that the price was still most reasonable. The funds were released two hours ago—the King's money, of course—but your majesty, look at their value. They are a match for some of the finest jewels in the crown's possession."

"They *are* the finest jewels in the crown's possession," Nitti whispered in a trembling, enraged voice.

Joe was dumbfounded, but the Prime Minister's eyes were ablaze. He whispered again, his words becoming raspy as his anger increased.

"They *were* ours—*already* ours—you stupid lout. They belonged to us. We gave them to—to—and you paid King's money for them again?"

Nitti choked off, more from rage, Joe thought, than from the realization that his words were indiscreet. His hands were trembling, and involuntarily he clutched at the open purse.

The shock of all this was enough to make Joe want to wash his hands of his new role as King. Could it be that the Earth girl was still alive? The thought of that brought a smile to Joe's face. He wanted to leave—he wanted to leave and find her. But no—for the moment he *was* the King. He had the power to make decisions, and as long as the crowd believed him to be their King, what could Nitticello do?

Joe leaned to the microphone.

"I have an important, official announcement for all the people of Karridonza."

The Prime Minister started squirming in his seat at this. Joe rambled on.

"Please listen to my words closely. Two days ago—as a royal gesture of friendship—the kingdom bestowed rich gifts of jewelry to a visitor from another planet, just as she was preparing for her departure. But we now find that these gifts have been sold back to us. We believe it's possible this woman may still be on our world, perhaps injured, perhaps masquerading as a peasant woman. If this is true, we must do everything we can to find her."

"Yes," Nitti joined in, the anger in his voice barely controlled. "She may be undermining our institutions."

Joe snatched the microphone away from him. "This woman may be wandering about our countryside in a daze as the result of an air spinner accident. She had departed in an automatic spinner, but the spinner never returned to the palace from the skystation. We believe it may have crash-landed in the storm—"

"S-s-sh! We'll investigate these matters in due time," Nitti whispered again. "Get *on* with the ceremony."

"And so, ladies and gentlemen of Karridonza," Joe went on, lifting his hand dramatically and pointing to the condemned man on the bench, "we are going to use all means at our disposal to find this woman from Earth. This slave whom we are about to execute is also from Earth. It is possible—however unlikely—that he may be able to help us in some way."

"What are you driving at?" Nitti gasped.

"I hereby declare," Joe sang out to the breathless audience, "that this man's execution must be postponed."

CHAPTER TWELVE

JOE'S command over the Sashes was unquestioned. The audience may have been disappointed, but there wasn't much evidence of it, for everyone was curious over the King's speech regarding an Earth woman masquerading as a peasant. Everyone in the crowd could reflect that they had seen a peasant woman somewhere along the way who might have been the mysterious Earth visitor in question. And what was it that Nitticello's words had hinted about her undermining the Karridonzan institutions? Upon this point there would be plenty of talk behind closed doors. What a townsman or an interplanetary trader might think about slavery was not a thing to be aired in the King's courtyard.

The condemned man was led back to the palace.

Nitti was white—chalky white. There was a vile poison in his eyes. His fingers were twitching. He was going to kill someone quick, Joe thought.

He was right at Joe's side as they marched back to the palace. Sashes were all around them, much to Joe's relief. There wasn't a chance for anyone to say anything.

But just wait till that gag is removed from the King's mouth, Joe thought. That would uncork a nice stream of wildfire. No, Nitti couldn't let that happen. He'd either stage a phony confrontation with the condemned "slave" or simply murder him outright to save his own hide. And Nitti wasn't a man to sell one square inch of his hide. Not while he was doing so well lining his pockets with the precious gems and riches of others.

What if the royal court found out? The very thought gave Joe a pounding headache. Nitticello would be a dead man. He knew it, too. You could sense it in his hurried step.

Up the yellow walk in stiff formation, Sashes on either side, the condemned man was forced along at the head of the procession.

Up the steps to the plaza. Past the row of torch lanterns. Through the columns. Up more marble steps. Then the palace reception room—what were all those people waiting for? Conferences with the King, no doubt.

Nitti a dead man? What about Joe Peterson? He was on a powder keg of his own. As an imitation king he had now cooked his own goose, so to speak. Would Nitticello ever trust him again? No—not even if he behaved like a perfect puppet for weeks and weeks. He had made his bold move, saving the King from execution. He would never have another chance to open his mouth.

And still, temporarily the crown was his. The Sashes didn't know, and as long as they didn't know, they would step lively at his slightest order.

Supper was served. You could tell from the way the kitchen workers walked on tiptoe and gave each other the furtive eye that they knew something was amiss. They could certainly see that the Prime Minister was white with rage about something. Nitti's tray waited while he ran through his medicines. He was fixing another hypodermic needle.

It was just as well, Joe thought, that the King was pretty thoroughly doped. After another needle, Nitticello removed the gag from Arvo's mouth, and he was seen to be in a satisfactory condition. Comfortable enough, but too soggy with drugs to start throwing any accusations around. He seemed to know that he had narrowly escaped death, but he thought it was better to sleep than start bragging about it. Much better to sleep than to be King.

Both Stobber and Nitti kept a close eye on the situation; but Joe did what he could to guarantee that they wouldn't take matters into their own hands. He ordered two Sashes and a court officer to stand by the "slave" until further notice.

This done, he finished his supper hastily and went out into the reception room to fare some of his troubled subjects.

"Remember your throat," Nitti said to him, practically grinding his teeth into crumbs. "You're in no condition to talk."

"You'd better come along to make sure I don't," Joe said, adjusting his regal uniform. "If you can give them the answers, I'll nod my agreement. Yes?"

"No."

"Then what shall I tell them? If they want the court to help pay someone's funeral expenses because the lavender vine visited them with death, what shall I tell them?"

"You accompany him, Stobber," Nitti said. "Make them understand that his throat has gotten even worse and that he must refuse all requests for the time being."

LATE that night Joe Peterson rolled his bed over against the open window and flopped down, a thoroughly fatigued king. He propped his elbows on the windowsill and stared out at the black night.

He had taken the precaution to arm himself, earlier in the evening, and had found a friendly Sash who was willing to

demonstrate his own skill with a ray pistol for the King's benefit. The Sash hadn't guessed that he was giving Joe Peterson a
lesson in the use of a Karridonzan weapon.

Now, with ray pistol at hand, Joe looked out at the night and
wondered what mysteries the darkness held. He would try not
to go to sleep as long as anyone was stirring in the palace. His
life seemed as uncertain as a puff of thistle down, tossed in the
breeze.

Had the attendants of the King become suspicious? For all
his excuse of illness, his manners must have given him away
many times. How could he have forgotten where he kept his
own ray pistols? Why should he have stammered over little
decisions regarding what clothing he would wear tomorrow?
Why had he dodged the simple exercise of signing his name to a
court note?

It was a terrific relief to be alone, at last. The Sashes on the
night shift would play cards outside his door all night, no doubt,
but at least no one would barge in without first stirring a
commotion—unless they came in by way of the window. That
darkness—it was something Joe Peterson had never been afraid
of before. But tonight the whole hillside around the fortress
abounded with people who had made camp for the night. They
didn't want to return to the valley until morning. When
Nitticello had ordered them to clear the grounds and go on
home, they had only moved outside the limits of the courtyard,
and there had bedded down to wait for morning.

Now there were a few stars piercing through the clouds. Joe
felt better. He leaned a little farther out the window and tried to
discern the marble ledge down below. He reached down to
discover that it was only a foot and a half below his windowsill.
Beneath it were the windows of the lower floor, he recalled—
high arched windows divided by marble columns. But no light
emerged from them, and the ledge extended outward far enough
to cut off the view.

That ledge would be a perfect catwalk for a prowler, he
thought. He tried to dismiss that fancy from his mind. Again

he rested his arms on the sill and closed his eyes.

Presently he thought he heard a light swishing sound from the ledge. He laughed to think how he'd kidded himself into imagining he had really heard something.

He opened his eyes. He saw nothing. Just the black shadowy ledge.

Swisssssh!

It was real. He could hear it but he couldn't see it. Then the long stripe of blackness directly beneath his gaze began to emerge into something purple, like an immense luminous rope. It was there, lying in gentle curves along the ledge.

A blotch of black broke the length of it a few yards away. The blotch of blackness was moving, and it was causing the low swishing noise.

And then, to Joe's consternation, the luminous rope went out.

All was blackness again. Then...

Swissssssh!

Still nothing to be seen. But the thing was closer. Then came a whisper, almost directly beneath Joe's elbows.

"Slave...are you there, slave?"

"Pudge!" Joe gave a tight gulp. "Pudge, you scary devil...what are you doing there?"

"Dragged my feet so you'd hear me coming. I just dropped in to pay my respects to the new king."

"Come in off that ledge. The lavender vine was right there just half a minute ago. It started to turn visible and then it went out again."

"It's still here," said Pudge. "I'm riding on it. It just now brought me up."

Joe's blood froze again. The thing was there—invisible.

PUDGE crawled in the window and hopped onto the bed. "Your majesty! I saw your performance at the execution grounds this afternoon. You were magnificent."

Pudge's talk was welcome. His presence always warmed

Joe's spirits, and just now Joe's spirits needed warming as never before. But Joe couldn't converse normally as long as he believed there was a branch of the lavender vine lying invisible right out side his window.

"What happened to it? Is it still there?"

"Well, if I were you, slave...I mean, your *majesty*...I wouldn't reach my hand down. It's waiting there...waiting to take me back. I won't stay but a minute."

Joe drew his arms back from the windowsill. He mentioned that he had brought a ray pistol along for safety. But Pudge only laughed.

"A ray pistol means nothing to the lavender vine. Now...what I came to tell you...your *majesty*...is that you may not be King very much longer. So try to enjoy it while you can."

"That's why I have this pistol."

"Well, I can't guarantee they'll attempt to snuff your life out without giving some kind of fair warning. However, even though your death is definitely a big part of their future plans, I don't think they'll be bothering with you just yet. For the moment it's King Arvo they're fixing their designs on."

"How do you mean?"

"Well, it seems that Nitti's plan for exchanging you two boys didn't work out quite as well as he had hoped. Just when he thought he had you dangling on a string, it seems that you got up on your hind legs and walked off with the show. Very pretty, my boy," Pudge chuckled. "Very pretty, but not safe. In that one moment you reduced your puppet value from priceless to something less than zero. And there *has* to be a king."

"But the real King Arvo knows what they've pulled," Joe responded. "In another minute he'd have been turned into burned ozone. How can they ever expect to put him back into their harness of control?"

"Drugs. Hypnotism. Suggestions and ideas that will prey on his weaknesses and confuse his sick thoughts. By the time he comes out of it they're going to have him believing that he dreamed up all of this king-switching business himself. Dreamed it up after he'd been "accidentally" bumped on the head by Stobber when they were inside your cell. And they're going to make him believe that all of the happenings at the execution were real, except with the characters interchanged."

"They'll make him believe he changed his mind at the last minute and saved *me*?"

"That's right, slave. Oops…I did it again…I mean, your *majesty*. They'll tell him he was looking down at the victim as though he was imagining the poor fellow's plight—and that he was out of his head all of the time, imagining that he was the very fellow he intended to execute." Pudge chuckled again. "Quite a story, isn't it?"

"Good lord," Joe muttered. "Can they make it stick?"

"That's what they're going to try—you can wager on it. Then there's the issue of the lavender—"

Pudge stopped in mid sentence and grew quiet for a few moments. His thoughts were racing with all of the knowledge he had acquired about the lavender vine bedlam of the past several nights. He had observed how the lavender vine's nightly sieges had all at once become the talk of the kingdom. The old timers were saying that there had never been a siege like this before. The Prime Minister had publicly dismissed these concerns, though, stating that the old timers always made these kinds of statements whenever the lavender vine stretched out for a few "growing exercises" up and down the valley. But this time it was much worse. It was coming to a real crisis. If the King's fortress was to stand solid and the Prime Minister was to prosper, something would have to be done.

"The point is," Pudge finally said, "the lavender vine is something Nitti has never been able to understand. King Arvo has an ability of control that Nitti doesn't have. And Nitti is going to try to extract that secret before he dissolves Arvo into nothingness. That's why Nitti and Stobber will try their best to hoax the King out of his real memories of what happened this afternoon." A playful smirk came over Pudge's face. "At least that's their plan for the moment…"

"What do you mean?" Joe asked, a look of puzzlement on this face.

"They will have to *find* him first," Pudge said with yet another chuckle. "They don't know it yet, but when morning comes they're going to find him *gone*."

"What? Gone? How do you know?"

"Just a little joke on my part. I turned him loose—the lavender vine assisting—about ten minutes ago." Pudge gave a laugh that was definitely froggish, then he added, "Well, I'd better go or I'll lose my ride. Don't shoot till I get out of range…your *majesty*. Bye-bye."

CHAPTER THIRTEEN

IN one of the darkened camps within a mile of the fortress, six persons huddled around the dying coals of a campfire. They had become only shadowy figures to each other; and yet, with one exception, each one knew the other as well in the dark as if they were under floodlights.

The single exception was Marcia Melinda. She was the newcomer who, with one act of devotion, had won the inner circle's confidence.

Around the fire they were awaiting the return of two other members of the inner circle—two men who had volunteered to undertake a daring reconnoitering mission to the King's palace.

Nadoff, the merry, round merchant, was speaking. He was more buoyant than ever tonight. Things had gone much better than anyone had anticipated.

"To think that we turned the treasure in the nick of time—we have the King's money! And—the King's own agent arrived in time to upset the execution. The cause of freedom has gathered great power on this day. Miss Melinda, we could all hug you."

Marcia Melinda blushed at this.

"Oh, you needn't be embarrassed. We won't actually hug

you, my dear…though you'd better keep a stern eye on our younger members, even though you've tried to disguise yourself as an older woman. Eh…Starwold? Eh…Mazoweb? Ah…but you needn't answer. I am simply beside myself with rejoicing."

Suddenly a noise in the distance caught the merchant's ear.

"But listen…" Nadoff said as he cocked an ear. "Do you hear someone coming?"

Nadoff's high spirits didn't prevent him from keeping a deft ear and a clear view of the evils that haunted every slavery fighter in the realm. After a few moments of silence, he went on…

"No, Miss Melinda and brothers, we mustn't be misguided by the King's act. He postponed an unjust execution—yes. But don't let that soften your feelings toward him. Why did he do it? Because he believes this fellow will help him find Miss Melinda. Not out of a sense of mercy."

"You have good reason to be cautious, Nadoff," Mazoweb reminded the leader. "By this time they're on your trail for selling the jewels. They'll guard your shop and arrest anyone who comes asking for you."

"We've started our plans circulating," Nadoff said. "The time to strike is near at hand."

"S-s-sh."

Marcia could hear soft footsteps approaching. At a short distance from the campfire the returning operatives identified themselves. Nadoff stirred the coals. The dim light barely outlined them. Not two—but three.

Two of them were the men who had been sent on the reconnoitering mission.

The third was the tall, broad-shouldered "slave" who had so narrowly missed his execution that afternoon.

King Arvo looked around at the strange group of people and knew that these were some of his less fortunate subjects. He was full of confused feelings about what had happened through this terrible day. He was furious with the Prime Minister—Nitti, the traitor! He was seeing so much red that the firelight before his eyes paled in comparison.

But these people thought of him as a slave. And they believed they had rescued him from an eventual execution. They were right on that count. It could have been murder tonight as easily as execution earlier in the day.

They were imploring him to speak. If only he could get his mind off Nitticello and listen to what they were saying. They wanted information—they wanted inside news from the palace. However, since he was too groggy to enter any kind of discussion, they allowed him to lie down and rest, warming his face at the low fire.

They continued to talk about him. However, this time they spoke of him not as a rescued slave, but as King Arvo. There was much hatred against the King. The awfulness of his situation ate at him. He came up on his elbows, looked around at their intense, determined faces. They were planning a rebellion!

They had rescued him from the King...from himself. And they were going to make the King and Nitticello pay for their crimes against the people. This was a rare occasion indeed—the enemies of the King confiding in him.

Then he rested his gaze upon the lovely peasant woman. She

was speaking. That voice…it was Marcia Melinda!

She was not dead? What had happened?

She began speaking to him. She was speaking to him in the belief that he was the American slave.

"You must help us fight against the palace. Can you promise me that?" she asked him. "Later there may be a chance for both of us to return to Earth—but we must win our battle against slavery first."

He blurted, "You're not dead—"

"Ah, he talks," said the deep-throated Nadoff. "He's coming out of it."

"No…I'm not dead," Marcia Melinda was smiling through her disguise. "So you knew that the King and the Prime Minister tried to kill me? Well…they missed their chance. I knew they would never allow me to reach the skystation alive, so I parachuted down before the beam struck my air spinner. Minutes later it crashed, but I was already on the ground unharmed."

King Arvo exhaled a deep breath of relief. "Thank the stars." he mumbled. It was if a great weight had been lifted from his shoulders. He sat up. He stared at his slave clothes and passed his hand over his head. What a peculiar feeling it was, the American hairstyle they had fixed on his head. The Earth girl wouldn't know his real identity. After all, she had seen the American slave for only a few minutes. He had given his name as Joe Peterson; she had asked the King to let him accompany her; and then when she was about to depart, she had kissed him, rather tenderly, Arvo thought.

"And she thinks I'm Joe Peterson," he whispered under his breath. "She remembers that one minute of friendship."

Arvo took a curious delight in this thought, but he was alarmed by their discussions of revolt against the King.

"I know you'll want to help us," Marcia was saying, "after all you've been through."

"You want me to help fight the King?" Again he looked at his costume of slave rags. He swallowed hard.

"How about it, my friend?" Nadoff asked him pointedly. "Are you willing?"

"It's a strange idea," Arvo said uncertainly.

"There's nothing strange about it. If you've been through as much as the average slave, you needn't use today's narrow escape as an added incentive. You must certainly know how all slaves feel. Haven't you been beaten the same as the others of your kind?"

THEY started to examine his bare back for striped scars of the whip, but he resisted, turning to the light.

"I suppose I've been through as much as many slaves have."

"I knew how you'd feel," said Marcia. "Free American citizens don't knuckle down to slave masters. What was your name—Joe? Joe Peterson? You're uncomfortable and tired, aren't you? Maybe these men can offer you a blanket. And food—are you hungry?

It wasn't like the elaborate care he was used to at the palace, but it was the best they had to offer, and he was grateful—deeply grateful to be in the hands of friendly people.

Friendly? Only because they believed he was Joe Peterson. Imagine if he had told them the truth. They would probably be as eager to kill him as the Prime Minister himself. They could win their revolt in a single moment by forcing him—at the point of a knife—to concede to their demands.

Or would he be able to summon a few squads of loyal Sashes and have them executed on the spot?

Execution? That word stabbed through King Arvo with an entirely new meaning. He had almost been on the receiving of it earlier in the day—an execution ordered by the King himself. It had become an ugly word all at once. And it used to be such a convenient word.

They smothered their fire and gathered their camp things together. It was time to get on. The dawn mustn't find them this close to the fortress grounds.

They hiked through the darkness. Marcia was at Arvo's side,

and they both stayed close within the small party. Arvo didn't want to miss a word of what was being said.

"You're not well," Marcia had commented. "You don't seem the same. But I can understand, especially after what you've been through."

Yes, and if she had known who he was and what he was going through now—

As they walked on, the two men who had rescued him began speaking, retelling the account of their long vigil around the palace. They had apparently watched the Prime Minister and the "King" all through the evening hours. But at length there had been an unaccountable piece of luck. Apparently someone had released the American prisoner by mistake and allowed him to wander out onto the grounds—someone who looked like a cross between a boy and a frog, obviously one of the freakish victims of the lavender vine.

Arvo couldn't refrain from asking a question. "You say you watched the King?"

"Certainly we watched him."

"What was he doing?"

"Talking with officials and townsmen and slave-masters around a conference table."

"What did he tell them?"

The men became somewhat elusive at this point. "It was hard to hear very much, but from what we could tell the King said very little. He complained of a sore throat."

Marcia, hiking along at Arvo's side, touched his arm meaningfully. "He was probably waiting for Nitticello to give him the answers."

"Oh…is that the King's way?" Arvo asked.

"He's always yielding to the Prime Minister," Marica responded. "If he ever did anything else, Nitticello would probably turn the palace upside-down."

"The King must be very weak," said Arvo.

Marcia answered carefully. "I'm not sure it's entirely weakness. My impression is that the King began his reign by being too kind and considerate, and clearly...too indecisive. Nitticello took advantage of this right from the beginning. Frankly, there were many things about the King that I liked during my stay at the palace. He has a certain quiet strength, I believe, that he's never been able to find within himself."

Nadoff cleared his throat. "Careful what you say about such a scoundrel."

"But I believe it," said Marcia. "Haven't I a right to say what I believe?"

"The King is our sworn enemy," said Nadoff. "As long as there's a slave in Karridonza I have no use for the King. He's almost as much of a monster as the Prime Minister. Look what he's done to this poor fellow."

At this point Arvo Arvadello's mind succumbed. It had taken the words of a few common villagers to make him understand what a truly awful, insensitive, indecisive ruler he had become. These poor villagers who wanted nothing more than to live in peace, who feared for their lives at the very thought of the Prime Minister's wrath. The traitorous Prime Minister who had controlled the King in the same manner that a puppeteer controls a marionette. He suddenly felt enveloped by an overpowering sense of guilt. And even if these people killed him on the spot, he could not continue the charade any longer.

"Stop," Arvo said. "Light a lantern. Please."

"What's the matter?" Nadoff asked. He stopped the party and someone lit one of the lanterns. "What's wrong?"

"Hold the light up to my face," Arvo said. "Look at me...look at me closely."

They moved into the light and stared intently at Arvo's face.

"Closer still," he implored. "I'm not the slave you believe I am. I'm not Joe Peterson. I am—" he stammered momentarily before choking out the words, "I am...the King."

"What?" Nadoff gave a deep disbelieving scowl. He shook his head slowly.

"Believe me...I *am* King Arvo."

There were stares of disbelief from all.

"I—I had to tell you," Arvo said, his voice trembling. "I couldn't let this go on any longer. I'm so sorry…I'm so sorry for everything."

There was a short moment of silence that seemed to go on for an eternity.

"Poor fellow," Nadoff finally said, looking to Marcia. "The strain has been too much."

At that the rest of the men then burst into soft laughter.

After several seconds Nadoff quieted them. He looked at the King with pitying eyes. "I've seen an overwrought slave do this very same thing once before. Last year at the upper end of the valley. It was a tragedy—seeing a mind snap like that. Don't worry, my friend…we'll take care of you."

Marcia looked at Arvo intently, cutting him with her steady, penetrating eyes. "I don't know…"

"Put out the light," Nadoff cut in. "We've not time to loiter." And they hiked on into the night.

CHAPTER FOURTEEN

THEY moved westward along the crest of the ridge above the valley. Dawn came. They descended into the shadows and kept going.

The day brought several perilous encounters with other travelers. Some, like themselves, were returning from the execution that didn't happen. And if any of these travelers were known to be in sympathy with the revolt, there were warm exchanges of plans and confidences.

But the reports came from all directions that groups of Sashes were out on a search for the "peasant woman" who had turned her gifts into cash for the benefit of the rebels.

Scouts moved over the land in fortress air spinners, and Nadoff and the others were continually on the alert to hide Marcia and themselves whenever searchers came their way. Marcia exchanged her peasant woman's outfit for the clothing of a townsman, so there was less likelihood that scouts, flying over, would guess there was a woman in the party. She changed her make-up, and hid her hair under a cap.

But with the best of precautions, however, they couldn't avoid the net completely. A court automobile rounded the corner, where the road passed through a wooded area, and it was upon them before they could hide.

It was loaded with Sashes, looking tough and belligerent. The King gulped. He saw the number as the car approached. He knew the captain of the outfit. Was it possible that he himself wouldn't be recognized?

Before he could get his wits together, Nadoff was snapping, "Down, you. Be tying my shoe. I'm your master."

The King obeyed. By the time the car came alongside, Nadoff, his back turned to the highway, was bending to direct the "slave." He was tongue-lashing him. In fact, he was cursing him. The King was stung by it all. He wasn't used to being ordered around. But Nadoff knew what he was doing. He gave the King a slap across the head, and the King staggered back, more from surprise than pain.

It was just enough to distract the Sashes from their purpose; and later Nadoff explained that there was nothing that could divert Sashes so effectively as a slave-beating scene.

"They've done so much of it themselves that the sight of it draws them like a magnet. I hated to strike you, Joe…Joe Peterson. I know you're sick and your mind's a little dizzy. But you saw how it worked."

It had worked. The Sashes evidently assumed that Nadoff was a slave master. It was rebels they were looking for. They stopped one of the straggling members of the party long enough to ask if he'd seen a girl disguised as a peasant woman, or if he knew a merchant named Nadoff. His answers were elusive enough. And Marcia, trembling in her disguise as a man, took their glares without wincing. The car then backed up and one of the Sashes jumped out and gave the King three sharp lashes with a whip. This satisfied the lot of them so they drove on.

"I'll have them in chains," the King muttered to himself

stubbornly as the party moved along.

"You can't let a little whipping like that bother you," Nadoff said. "Under that delusion yet? Still think you're King Arvo himself?"

"He may *be* the King," Marcia said in a low whisper.

"No king is a king unless he's wearing the official robes," Nadoff said. "Joe Peterson, I'm not saying that you don't have kingly qualities. But these Sashes aren't impressed by men. They're impressed by crowns. Just lucky for you they were looking for a woman and not an escaped slave."

"We're going to have to hide, aren't we…your majesty?" Marcia whispered, looking through him.

"Yes," King Arvo said, smearing the bleeding lines across his side. "We'll hide long enough for me to take a lesson in being a slave. There are many things about it that I need to know."

CHAPTER FIFTEEN

IN the palace of the King's fortress, high noon shone through the shiny glass windows and lighted the red goblet on the tray that had been set before Joe Peterson, "Acting King."

Joe had decided not to drink the wine that had been served with his luncheon. When the attendant came in, Joe offered it to him, and the attendant downed it at one gulp and was very well pleased over the favor all day long.

Joe's refusal of the wine was an index to his case of the jitters. He knew instinctively that things would soon come to a head.

"I damn well wish I could make something happen," he mumbled to himself. And he was thinking in terms of his temporary crown. It was a haunting sensation, being in power. But it wouldn't last, he thought. Already Nitticello had learned what a complete failure Joe had turned out to be in his role as a kingly puppet. The sore throat hadn't kept Joe from talking. After the recent conferences with some of the townspeople, the rumor was going the rounds that three or four important citizens of the kingdom had discovered they would rather do business with the King than with the Prime Minister.

"No, it can't last long," he mumbled again.

He looked out the window. Six times this morning he had looked down at the ledge, wondering whether the lavender vine was there, still in its invisible state. Twice he had actually reached down to the ledge and brushed his hands along the stone. Now he was tempted to try it again.

He slipped through the window and allowed his feet to dangle toward the ledge. *Swish!* His elbows skidded off the sill and he fell. He tried to catch himself on the ledge—a mad flurry of flailing limbs. His hands missed!

They missed because he was being lifted.

He swung upward through the air, caught in the clutches of a power he couldn't see. He looked back at the receding palace. Under the noon sun, the trail of lavender was barely visible. The vine was carrying him out over the valley. "Hi there, slave. How's your majesty? Didn't know you had company, did you?"

And there was Pudge, sliding down what must have been an arm of the vine, though Joe couldn't see it.

"Pudge…where are you taking me?"

"I'm taking myself down to the marshes. Come along?"

"No. Take me back."

"Talk to the vine, don't talk to me," Pudge answered. Then with a weird froggish laugh right up the harmonic scale and down again, "Don't look so scared, my friend. You're the King, you know."

"That's why I need to get back—"

"That's why you need to go out and visit your people. So long, King."

The vine bent low, a hazy ribbon waving over the green marshes. Pudge swooped over the surface, let go and dived into the water with a happy splash. Then Joe was being carried on— up and up—across the ridges to the west of the fortress. For the first time, after his many months of enslavement, he was getting a bird's eye view of the kingdom.

AFTER several minutes of riding westward, crossing under clouds that made the vine momentarily visible, he began to descend. It was like an invisible slipperslide. He tried to hold on. The vine took that responsibility out of his hands. The substance was as steamy as a rope of cloud.

Down, down a long curved sloping course—and then the vine grew stouter. It gathered around him like pillows and bore him up just enough to break his fall.

Thump.

His two feet struck the ground just below a low cliff. And there was Marcia Melinda!

She gave a gasp of fright. "Good heavens!" Her hands came up to her cheeks. "It's—it's *you!*" She was staring wide-eyed at his clothes, his royal boots, his medals, his false mustache, and spade-shaped beard. "Or is it you?"

"Yes," Joe answered. "Yes, it's me...Joe...remember? Joe Peterson, the slave."

"Good lord it's all true then." She put her hand to her breast, became weak-kneed, and for a moment Joe thought she would crumble to the ground. She finally gathered herself up.

"You have me almost—speechless. I—I really don't know what to say." She took a long, deep breath. "Here I am wandering the countryside, when a slave in the King's robes is deposited on the ground in front of me." She started to laugh a little, her eyes still wide with astonishment. "You see, I just talked with the real King a few minutes ago. He was so worried that he didn't have a royal costume. But everyone else in our party thinks he's delusional. Even I didn't know whether to believe his story or not—and now you! Out of nowhere! Where in the world Joe Peterson did you come from?"

He dodged the question for the moment and gave her the questioning eye of a guest who isn't sure whether he should have dropped in. This apparently was a hiding place of some sort—a small alcove in the low cliff. A few yards farther down were other depressions in the soil and he guessed, from the distant mumble of voices in that direction, that a party of fugitives from justice had made camp here.

"Nice bit of scenery you have here," he observed. "You're probably far enough from the highway that you ought to be safe. Are you traveling alone? I mean you and the King?"

"No. I'm sure you can hear the voices of the others just as well as I can." Her expression became quite serious. "Can I trust you, Joe Peterson—can I?"

He shrugged and raised his eyebrows. He certainly hoped she could trust him. He wasn't telling her, but the very sight of her sent a mild thrill through him. She had beautiful hair, he thought. She had been combing it when he dropped in. She was dressed in the clothes of a townsman, but even dressed as a man she looked wonderfully feminine to him.

"Yes...you can trust me," he finally answered.

"Of course," she said. "After you saved the King's life from Nitticello, out there on the execution grounds—"

"Were you there?"

"I was hiding beyond the grounds, waiting."

"How did you know it was me?"

"I didn't know for sure until this very minute," she said, looking intently at him. "You traded places, of course—I should have known..."

"The Prime Minister traded us. We didn't really have any say in the matter."

"It's must have been awful, caught up in the scheme of an evil wretch like Nitticello. I always knew he'd do something desperate if the King ever asserted his own power."

Joe's throat tightened. "You and the King must be getting pretty well acquainted, aren't you?"

She tossed her head, and her hair fell over her shoulder. "What do you mean by that question?"

"Would you like to see him back in his rightful place?"

"I'm not sure. That's a question that requires much thought. It is his throne. And just in the past few hours I've come to learn that he may not be quite the monster we think he is.

Underneath all his weaknesses I believe he has a good heart. Yes, I'm getting acquainted with him, and I believe I'm beginning to like him."

Joe turned and edged away uncomfortably. He looked toward the shadows of the trees that overhung the cliff, wondering whether the lavender vine was still there.

Then her hand was on his arm and she was looking up at him smiling. "I don't know where you came from, but I'm terribly glad to see you again. I've been thinking about you."

Her words warmed him.

"The lavender vine brought me. That's how I got here. It's invisible at times. I think it must have brought me this way because I was wanting to see you again."

"Yes?"

"Yes," Joe said thoughtfully. "I don't quite understand how, but I think the vine can sense a person's thoughts and desires. The story of how I even came to be a passenger on it is a strange one. It involves an odd little fellow named Pudge. He's a froggish sort of a creature—completely indigenous to this planet, and..." Joe chuckled softly, "...most amusing at times." Joe's expression then turned wistful. "He's probably been the closest thing to a friend that I've had on this planet. At any rate, after I was carried off by the vine, I started thinking about escaping from this world, of getting myself over to the skystation. I suppose I thought I could use my charade as the King to somehow board a rocket bound for Earth. It was probably a hair-brained idea. The vine might have taken me there, though. In fact it was taking me in that general direction, but then..." Joe looked at Marcia and smiled, "...my thoughts turned to you." He caught her arms in his hands, drawing her a little closer. "You want to go back to Earth, too, I'm sure." Joe tilted his head slightly and smiled again. "I was thinking I'd like to take you with me."

SHE was a keen looking person, he thought, meeting his eyes that way, not fearing him, nor yielding to him against her will—just trying to know him; trying to gauge his strength and the sureness of his purpose.

"You don't belong here," he said.

"I've found a purpose here," she said slowly. "It's as important to these people as any of our Earth problems are to us. I'm beginning to feel as if I have a place here."

"The lavender vine is out there somewhere," he said, and then his voice was soft. "Let's go together—you and I—now."

"I'd like to—"

He drew her close and then he was kissing her, kissing her as if he had never known the sweetness of a woman before—as if this faraway world contained nothing for him but Marcia Melinda.

She was smiling a little as she drew away. "You didn't let me finish my sentence."

"You said you'd like to—"

"I'd like to—to think it over."

"Why?"

"The King, Joe...the King. We'd leave him—and the planet—in a dreadful lot of trouble if we were to simply leave now."

"I saved his foolish hide yesterday, didn't I? I'd think the rest should be up to him."

"They're not going to believe he's the King. He doesn't even look like the King right now. He looks terrible, and unless he has his royal robes and someone to identify him, he'll have trouble shedding his identity as Joe Peterson, condemned slave. And you know he's considered a runaway. The sentence for that is death. At any time they may find him and kill him."

Joe studied her coolly. Finally he said, "All right. Let me exchange clothes with him right now. Then, if you like, we're free—"

"Free? Free to do what? To be a slave again? That's what you'd be. I'm a fugitive myself. Do you think we could just waltz into the skystation and board a rocket for home? Think about it, Joe. If we can help the King, he may show his gratitude by helping us. And I can't possibly leave when so much is at stake for the people of this planet—especially the slaves. I believe King Arvo has the possibilities of being a decent ruler, but we have to give him that chance. In just the short time he's been in our company he's begun changing his opinions about slavery and executions. And I believe him to be sincere. I hope your not doubting me."

A resigned look came over Joe's face. "I'll go change clothes with him. Lead me into your friends' camp carefully, though. This is going to be quite a shock to them—especially the King.

Joe knew Marcia was right. They had to stay and do what they could for the King and his people. Strangely enough, Joe felt more worried about Marcia's feelings toward the King than the plight of the slaves. Could she have affection for him?

"Let's go," Joe said.

But as soon as Joe stepped out of the protection of the cliff, invisible fingers caught him and lifted him up toward the clouds once again.

The lavender vine!

The next thing he knew he was many miles away, dropping down into a steamy marsh. A voice spoke to him as his feet hit the soft, wet soil beneath him.

"Hello there, slave."

It was Pudge.

CHAPTER SIXTEEN

"WELCOME! Welcome!" Pudge called out to his friend from Earth. "Come in and join me. The water is fine for upset nerves."

"The lavender vine is taking over my life," Joe growled in frustration.

He picked himself up out of the clump of marsh grass and adjusted his kingly garments. It was easy enough for a creature that was half boy and half frog to splash around in those muddy waters, but it was not a place for a king to be dropped. He stepped from one grassy island to another until he reached a bank of dry earth.

Pudge followed him, his bright green skin shining through the water's surface as he swam alongside.

"You must have wanted to come here," Pudge said, "The vine must have sensed it. We're you trying to escape from something? Perhaps you wanted to walk out in the middle of a conversation or escape from a circumstance you were caught up in. After all, the vine did bring you here in a great hurry."

"Don't try to tell me the vine only does what I wish it to do," Joe said sourly. "I have a hunch that dozens of persons are wishing dozens of different, conflicting things all at once. How can any magical power serve everybody? Why would it have sensed only my thoughts?"

Pudge blinked his big green eyes and chortled to himself. Then Joe realized what had happened.

"Oh…I think I understand now. I was brought here because that's what *you* wanted. It was *your* wish. You probably said to yourself, 'Please, lavender vine, let Joe Peterson drop smack dab in the middle of this mud puddle.' Was that it?"

"Ugh," Pudge said.

"Guilty or not guilty?"

"You see," said Pudge, "the vine sometimes does nice favors for nice people. And it also does some mischief, too, just to keep freaks like me amused."

"Guilty or not—"

"Guilty…I needed a playmate."

"You might pick on someone beside the King. I am the King, you know—temporarily."

Joe had removed his boots to drain the water out of them and he dangled his feet in the pool. Pudge whistled at him and motioned him to take his feet out of the water.

"You won't be a king long if you spend your time in the water. I'd just as well let you in on the secret. When you've been riding around in the atmosphere on the lavender vine, you become susceptible."

"Susceptible? Susceptible to what?" Joe jerked his feet out of the water and dried them on the lining of his mud-splashed royal robe.

"Susceptible to change. You're in danger of changing into something that fits your thoughts or actions. That's how the change came over me. I thought it was a lot of fun...playing frog. The vine dropped me in here a long time ago. I was just a small boy then. I was splashing around—having the time of my life. I never guessed that I was beginning to...change. Then I felt the webs forming between my toes, the croakiness coming to my throat, and when I climbed out onto the bank—about where you're sitting right now—I saw that my skin had turned green and shiny. And that's how it happened. That's how your friend Pudge came into being."

"Good lord..." Joe got into his boots and began to hike away, glancing back at the marsh with a feeling of horror.

Pudge followed him. "Don't worry, I suspect you won't be turning into a frog the same way I did. After all, you have to be playing frog to be turned into a frog."

"No. I'm not playing frog."

"No, you're safe from webbed feet and green skin. But you have been playing king."

JOE stopped in his tracks. The words struck into his brain. Playing king? Yes, he had been. In fact, he had been swept away within the past hour by a strong desire to make the most of his crown.

"That can happen to anyone," the frog boy was rattling on. "As long as you're still soaked with the vine, you can easily bend into the thing you happen to be wanting."

Joe began to stride up the highway rapidly.

"What's the matter?" Pudge called after him. "Did I say the wrong thing?"

"I don't want to be anybody but Joe Peterson," Joe retorted.

He thought he heard a froggish chuckle. He hurried on. But all the way up the long slope he kept hearing it at intervals—the faint chortling of a mischievous frog-like boy.

He caught a ride with a court car loaded with Sashes who were returning from a day of scouring the countryside for the peasant woman and the escaped slave. They were astonished to find his highness wandering along a lonely highway in the middle of nowhere. He explained that he had gone for a long walk unattended. Being well-disciplined Sashes, none of them questioned his explanation. He was the King. They escorted him up the steps to the plaza, past the row of nine torch lanterns, and around the palace to a private entrance. It had been a disturbing afternoon. He was glad to get back into the seclusion of his private study.

Behind the locked doors, he began to think of Marcia. She had spoken of finding a place for herself in this world—a purpose. Well, maybe he'd make a place for himself too.

He selected one of the crowns from the shelf of the King's dressing room, walked to the mirror and tried it on. It was an informal crown of cloth, with a silken lining that rested softly over his narrow mane of hair. The ornaments were of precious stones, and their glitter in the mirror threw flashes of colored light around the room.

He stood gazing at himself, imagining the conference table with the palace officials and the officers from the several provinces sitting around, waiting for him to speak.

He heard a shuffling noise and whirled to see what it was…

Pudge again!

"Three more crowns on the shelf, your majesty, if you want to try them on for size."

"Pudge…you and your damned mischief! How did you catch up with me so quickly?"

"There's a ledge outside your window, and on it you will see—*ahem*—nothing. But it's there, slave. And that's why I'm here. Now if you'd like something in a solid gold crown—"

"S-s-sh! Don't say it."

"It's got you going, hasn't it? Come on, tell me. Where's the real king? Didn't you get to see him today? Or have they already cornered him and shot his heart out with a ray gun?"

Joe felt guilty. He put the crown back on the shelf.

"If they shoot him," Pudge said as he hopped up on a polished table, "You'll get to be king and the girl will be queen. And you could make me Prime Minister." he chuckled slightly. "I'd be just the fellow. Take 'em out and execute 'em, boys, I need diversion!"

"Stop it, Pudge. You've no grasp of the situation."

"Didn't you get to see the girl? I thought you were wishing—"

"I saw her and she's the most rebellious citizen in the kingdom. She's helping to organize a slave rebellion. It's enough to make any king quake in his boots."

"There you are," said Pudge with a knowing laugh. "The first lesson in being a king: you're in constant fear. Fear of revolution. Fear of assassination. Your best friend may murder you in your sleep. Shall I bring in the gold crown?"

But at that moment an attendant called to say that the Prime Minister wanted to see the King at once. Pudge shrugged, hopped to the window and disappeared.

CHAPTER SEVENTEEN

IT was a dinner to be remembered. Everything in the line of luxurious food that Joe had ever dreamed of was served. And the drinks—Karridonzan concoctions that made the servants look on jealously from the doorways while Nitticello himself filled the goblets—Joe had never known there could be such delights.

The pressure was descending upon him: the dinner, the elegance of service, the brilliance of it all—and Nitti's clever words.

"You have the chance to be such a king as Karridonza has never known before, slave. What you have seen here tonight is only a small sample of the luxuries that will be yours if you decide to play along with us."

Joe was thinking of it—seriously. Luxuries. Power.

Importance. The pleasure of handing out justice. A beautiful palace to live in. Unlimited service.

And a queen?

He shook his head, a little dizzy with it all. No, the person he'd want for queen would be out working with the common people, stirring up discontent over the imperfections of the King.

"What's the cost?" Joe asked, in the matter of fact manner of a customer asking for his check at a supper club.

Nitticello edged closer to him. "Just let me run the show my own way, that's all."

The words were straightforward enough, Joe thought, but he didn't like the gesture. Nitti had placed the point of the carving knife on Joe's wrist, and he added a little pressure with each word. Joe cleared his throat uncomfortably, and when Nitti failed to observe what was wanted, Joe removed the blade with his other hand.

"Oh...pardon me," said the Prime Minister.

"I'm slightly allergic to sharp knife blades," Joe said.

"You'll find them indispensable for dealing with your subjects," said Nitti. "The hour of decision is at hand. Within a very short time we shall have ended the life of a certain runaway slave—if you know whom I mean. So this will be a lifetime job for you—his one living double."

Joe took a deep breath. He rose, walked around his chair, paused to look at himself in the mirror, and thought, for some strange reason, of the ugliness of Karridonzan manes as compared to American haircuts. He sat down and planted a fist on the table.

"You're doomed, Nitti. I'd be a fool to tie myself to the apron strings of a doomed man."

"Who told you I was doomed, your majesty?"

"Who?" Joe tried to think. Had the frog boy said it? Or had it been the words of Marcia Melinda or one of her followers. "I believe it was a friend of mine from the marshes."

"The frog boy?" Nitti made a wry face. "You aren't serious.

What would a half-witted amphibian child know about my future?"

"I think he gets around," said Joe.

"He's nothing but a court nuisance. Spends his time loitering in the local swamps."

Joe looked at the Prime Minister quizzically. "Do you know where he originally came from?"

"He was the son of an old philosopher. His father used to keep books for the treasury—but he was a troublesome fellow who became too headstrong and had to be…dispatched. It seems he was over-scrupulous about the court's records of accumulated gold—taxes and such. Things have gone much smoother since we…replaced him. His son, the frog boy, had somehow gained secret knowledge about the lavender vine. He began riding it back and forth, all over the kingdom. One day it deposited him in the marshlands and left its curse upon him. He's now only useful as a whipping boy."

Joe nodded and was going to let it go at that. But his words had disturbed the Prime Minister.

"Just what did he say to you about me? About my being…doomed?"

Joe shrugged. "If he's only half-witted, what's the difference?"

"What…what did he say? Why am I—in his foolish mind—doomed?"

JOE tried to recall. Some wisps of the afternoon's conversation came back to him. "He said you were doomed because you don't know how to control the vine."

Nitticello's fingers twitched at this and Joe noticed he had suddenly become tense.

"Go on."

All at once Joe's newly found powers were working. He was a king and a diplomat and a statesman, and he had opinions that people wanted to hear, including his corrupt Prime Minister. Yes, he would tell it to him straight.

"You're headed for destruction on two counts, Nitticello. One, your past cruelties are about to boomerang. The slaves are planning a rebellion, and I don't think you'll be able to stop it—unless you change things at once. Even then it may be too late."

"I've heard that before."

"Two. The people are restless over the actions of the lavender vine. It may be serving the court's wishes, but it's also terrorizing the people. Unless you can convince them that you have it under control, your house of cards is going to fall."

"So…" Nitticello wasn't even seeing Joe. He was looking off at the darkened sky beyond the plaza, and his fingers were knotted white. He ground his teeth and narrowed his eyes and mumbled something to himself. Then, facing Joe, he bit his words with decision. "All right. I'll show you. I'll control the vine. Once I've accomplished that, I'll end all the troubles. I'll clean the slate. I'll—"

Joe broke in with a follow-through bluff, and even as he spoke he half realized that he might be going too far. But if he could show that he already possessed a power that the Prime Minister didn't have—

"I already have the vine at my command." Joe said. "It's outside my window at this very moment."

"You? Why you young upstart. You're a foreigner. You can't possibly be serious. You're lying—*lying.*"

"Do you want to see it?" Joe was keeping a calm front, though his heart was pounding fiercely.

They went to his window. Joe pointed and said, "Watch it, and I'll make it perform."

Nitti bent to the window. "I don't see a damned thing."

"Turn around and you will," Joe said, reaching for the ray pistol on the bed table. "Up with those hands. Hold them high."

"Why, you sun-struck idiot. You damned sun-struck idiot." The Prime Minister's hands went up. His eyes were blazing a murderous fire that might have been a match for any ray gun, Joe thought. But Joe had him, and he knew it—the grandest of bluffs had worked.

"I'll kill you for this. I'll—"

"Save it. March this way." Joe gestured.

"Damn me if I won't make a torch out of you, and burn every fiber out of your—"

"Shut up. Into that corner...*now!* Move back—another step. Put your hands against the wall—"

Joe broke off with a gulp. An epaulette disappeared from his own shoulder, and a blast of air brushed the side of his arm. A strip of his sleeve disintegrated before his eyes. A silver stream of ray energy from the opposite side of the room was cutting an outline down the side of his body.

The mirror showed him—Stobber! Stobber held a white metal pistol as steady as starlight. One quaver of his hand would have melted a lung out of Joe's chest. Or cut his hip away. Or sliced into his brain.

In front of Joe, within three feet of Nitti, who stood facing the wall, the ray was drawing a path, shaped in lines of Joe's figures, in the plaster and stone of the partition.

"Relax, Nitti," Stobber called. "Try facing this way. It's all mine. Drop your gun on the table, slave."

Joe obeyed.

"That's fine," Nitti said, turning. "I counted on you. I gave this man a chance. It pays to know whether we can trust our new king. This makes twice that he's disappointed us."

THE ray blaze had disappeared. Joe turned to face the husky orange-sashed chief of the guards. As usual, the mane over his head was dyed with stripes of green and orange. For once Stobber wasn't wearing his adornments of emeralds. He hadn't wanted any flashes of light to give him away. As the two men talked, Joe gathered that he been under the strict watch of Stobber all evening. The two men were playing hand-in-glove, all right. The kingdom was in the palm of their partnership hand. All they needed was a fake king to keep up a front for them.

And all Joe needed just now was for Stobber to drop his guard for one split second.

They were leading him into his dressing room. He'd have to get out of those cut-away clothes before anyone else saw him. The Sashes would never be able to believe that there was a little war going on, right in the inner circle of the crown.

"Get that blue uniform on and be quick about it," Nitti snapped. "Keep him moving, Stobber. I'll see that the path is clear to the basement. What the palace folks don't know won't hurt them."

Nitticello's footsteps receded. Stobber's form filled the door of the dressing room. Joe hurried into a different uniform. What did they think they could do with him? The basement again? There'd never be a second escape from that dungeon, Joe thought. It would probably be quick death this time—if Stobber had his way.

Then, the one unguarded split second Joe had wished for came to pass. A noise in the outer corridor caused Stobber to glance away briefly. In that tiny moment Joe whirled and caught Stobber's gun arm. The ray blazed across the dressing room and cut a slice through dozens of suits and uniforms hanging there. The lower halves dropped with a swooshing noise. The ray was slicing in all directions, and it cut through the steel rod from which the uniforms hung. Three or four sections of the pipe fell, and Joe and Stobber were under them, struggling, rolling on the floor. For an instant Joe thought he had the ray pistol under control. Not so. It sliced down through the door, and half of the panel crashed to the floor.

Then the pistol went flying off into the other room, and the blaze of light had stopped. Stobber was up and charging as Joe rose to his knees. Joe caught his weight and went backward, his head crashing against the wall. A picture fell. Stobber fell too, for Joe had him by the legs, and then Joe was on him, punching him, and catching the fellow's sledge hammer fists in his own face.

They rolled into a corner where the King kept a collection of weapons. Stobber reached for a knife. Joe slugged him. He staggered and tried to get up. He was on knees and knuckles and he had a knife. But Joe pounced on him, and the knife clanged. They both scrambled for it—

Then the net of cable fell from the ceiling and they were both trapped under it. Nitti was in the doorway. He had pulled the cord. Above the weapon collection the metal net had hung, waiting to be tripped by the pull of a cord. It hung over both of them, and they couldn't fight against it.

"Now we've got him, Stobber," Nitticello said, an arrogant smile on his lips. He was rather pleased, Joe thought, that he had proved himself the master of the situation where the chief of the guards had failed.

"The way to the basement is clear."

CHAPTER EIGHTEEN

JOE gave a pained sigh. Too much exertion after a heavy meal, he thought. And here he was, a prisoner again in the basement cell where Pudge had previously come to his rescue.

He could hear the steps of the Prime Minister and his fiendish bodyguard shuffling away into silence. They weren't walking too spryly themselves, Joe thought. Neither one of them would feel like another fight for a few hours yet.

And on that theory, they probably assumed that he would fall asleep and rest quietly until they could figure out what to do with him.

That's where they were wrong. Joe went to work on the rock in the floor.

"That may be my own little secret," Joe said to himself. "Mine and Pudge's. I wonder—"

He pried at the stones. A new understanding of this exit had come to him. It was directly over the giant funnel. It had probably been formed originally, not by the builders of this fortress, but by the vine itself. The thing had no doubt pushed this rock out in the first place, for Pudge had certainly never been strong enough to lift it alone.

Joe's wish may have done it this time. Or it may have been the words he was chanting in his mind. The words he had heard the King utter earlier. "Seevia…Seevia…Seevia…"

The floor stone lifted with hardly any help from Joe. He placed it at one side of the opening, and sure enough, there was the whole magnificent tree of lavender light, rising up through the deep well, like a huge plant out of a colossal stone vase. One branch of the thing was whipping itself silently against the opening in Joe's floor.

He remembered how Pudge had coaxed it to come on through. He tried the motions, fanning at it with his hands. Within a minute or two his chains were cut. He was free? No, not quite. The steel door hadn't been left ajar this time.

For the next half-hour he worked in vain, trying to get the whipping arm of the vine to slide across to the door and cut its hinges.

It wasn't working. The vine seemed to have gone to its limit. It receded through the hole in the floor. He bent down to watch it.

"Pudge would leap for it," he said to himself. "Why shouldn't I?"

AS many times as it had carried him successfully, he shouldn't lack for confidence. And yet it would be like leaping into shafts of steam. Or ropes of cloud. It looked no more substantial than the stream of light that a searchlight sends into a foggy sky.

He lowered himself part way through the opening and hung there, supporting himself from the elbows. Now he saw the course he wanted to follow. If the large central trunk would catch him, he would slide from it to the down-sweeping branch on the left, and drop from it to a lower, flimsier looking arm beneath—and that one was pretty sure to bend with him and let him down over the steps. Not the deeper steps a hundred feet down, but the outer steps that were well out of danger from the center of the funnel.

From this point he would be able to make his way back into the palace, he thought. And he would go right to the headquarters of the Sashes. Yes, that would be the right maneuver. Stobber wouldn't be there. No, Stobber and the Prime Minister would be in some private chamber holding an all night conference. They had a "problem King" on their hands, and they'd be deciding what to do with him.

Joe chuckled. He'd turn the tables yet again tonight. Before the Sashes got wind of the trouble he'd have them under control.

But what about the vine? Could he control that too?

The vine had been quite good to him, he couldn't deny that, but it was still a monstrous thing that had killed many villagers. Joe knew he had struck a deep truth when he told Nitti that any ruler of this land was doomed if he couldn't make the vine serve him.

He lowered himself further and hung by the fingertips for a moment. The lavender light blazed in his eyes. Once more he traced his course mentally. The vine arms were moving slowly. He'd better make the leap now before they changed too much.

He dropped.

The steamy light passed through his hands. He was going down.

It wasn't catching him. And he wasn't catching it. He was falling straight for the center of the funnel. He scrambled wildly. He might as well have snatched at the air. He was falling. The series of white stone stairs that curved around in terraces, closing in toward the funnel's center, were slipping past him. He was falling straight and fast.

Down, down—now it was the vertical shaft around him, nothing else—down, down through the bottomless well of light.

CHAPTER NINETEEN

DOWN...down... He wasn't sure whether he was breathing. He began to wonder whether he was still falling. Or whether he was just suspended there. The steamy, luminous substance was simply racing past him, he thought. No, the white stone walls were flowing upward too, whenever he could catch glimpses of them. If he had spread his arms he might have burned his fingers on them.

Down...down...

The luminous substance was thickening. He was falling more slowly now. He lost the dread of striking solid bottom and feeling his life crushed out. He was coasting, leisurely...

And he was hearing sounds.

Sounds of human voices. Far away, yet close within the walls. A welter of little sounds. A confusion of many people talking at once. Scores of little conversations overlapping each other.

And his own breathing—the sound of it seemed magnified and it almost drowned out the faint little sounds. It was better if he held his breath. Yes, now he could hear the sounds more plainly. He seemed to have stopped falling when his breath was held. He breathed again—he was falling again, and again the echoes of conversations were tumbling over each other.

Presently he was finding a certain pattern to his fantastic situation. By breathing very slowly, even holding his breath, he lingered within range of certain conversations long enough to catch the essence of what was being said. He didn't understand what strange power the lavender vine had that allowed him to do this, but it was happening nevertheless.

Now he could hear the chant of numerous voices—the plaza. They were holding their religious rites up on the surface again tonight. And the lavender vine was sensitive to their religious songs. The voices began to fade as Joe took another breath. Then Pudge's voice came through, clear and strong.

Pudge was singing the religious songs too. Singing alone. And when Joe knew it was time to recite their prayers, he heard Pudge praying, too.

"Strange little fellow," Joe thought. And as he breathed again, he fell again. It was as though he was endlessly falling, then rising again. The lavender light flowed upward, and a hundred more voices chattered…rebel talk…fear of the vine…talk of escaping the Sashes…the outcry of a sleeping slave, dreaming he was being punished. Joe continued this for some time, holding his breath and listening to conversations—some extensively. Then one conversation in particular caught his ear. One of the voices was a woman.

It was the voice of Marcia Melinda.

Joe held his breath—deeply. Yes…it was Marcia talking with some other woman, confiding in her.

"If you could only help me make Nadoff understand and believe," Marcia was saying, "I would be so grateful. I've tried everything I can to convince him that the man we rescued is the King. I *know* he is. I think Nadoff doesn't want to believe it because he's beginning to like this fellow—and he has such a deep-rooted hatred for the King. So…you can see what I'm up against. I'm convinced the King may now be willing to help our cause."

The other woman said, "Not only do you believe him, but you're starting to believe *in* him, too. It seems you're also beginning to like him…"

"Yes, now that I understand him. He has certain qualities that a king needs. With the mere stroke of a pen he could make into reality what the rebels and slaves have dreamed about for ages. That is…if he were back on the throne—"

The Karridonzan woman prodded Marcia. "And if he had a good woman back of him?"

"Please don't misunderstand."

Joe was quivering, and his lips went tight.

"Do you mean you're not smitten with him?" the woman asked.

"I'm doing what I can to help him regain his confidence and to understand the plight of his people," Marcia said, "but I'm not thinking of affection in any way other than friendship."

"There's someone else then maybe? Someone else who's captured your heart? There must be. Is it the American you've been telling me about?"

Marcia's words were so quiet and so far away that Joe's heart almost stopped beating as he listened.

"The American is someone very special…" she laughed for a moment. "…in spite of his current appearance. He doesn't know it yet, but he has his teeth in my heart."

The woman murmured some sort of Karridonzan blessing. "Do you know him well?"

"I met him only recently. But a little frog-boy named Pudge has told me many things about him. This little Pudge goes everywhere and seems to know everything about everybody in the kingdom. I hope I'll see the American again."

Joe drew a deep, filling breath of air—and dropped away from the voice that had held him spellbound.

FOR many minutes the passing voices meant nothing to him. He wanted to close his eyes and simply fall, slowly and peacefully, through this mysterious well of light. This was a one way passage, he believed. It seemed unlikely that he would ever find his way out. And if this was to be all—if there should never be another glimpse of sunshine, or another conversation with living human beings, then he wanted those pretty words of Marcia to keep ringing—

A harsh note intruded upon his reverie.

It was the voice of Nitticello.

With half a breath, Joe stopped again. And before he had listened for more than a few seconds he discovered that the conversation seemed to be drifting along with him, so that he could breathe slowly without passing out of range.

It was a tense hour for Nitticello and Stobber, and Joe could feel the feverish eagerness with which they worked. They were searching for the secret of controlling the lavender vine.

"Here it is," Nitticello was saying. "On page one hundred twenty-eight. An old legend. Some old historian's theory."

"Read it," said Stobber. Joe could guess from the muffled words that Stobber was nursing a swollen face.

The Prime Minister read, "That which you give to others the vine also gives to you."

"Read on."

"Give the people bread, and the vine will give you bread."

"That's foolishness," Stobber growled. "Who gives us bread? The servants put it on the table, but the chefs prepare it, and the baker cooks it, and before that there's the slaves—they raise the grain and grind it."

"This, I think, would mean the vine would give the bread to the slaves," said Nitticello.

Joe could imagine he heard the grinding of teeth.

Nitticello read on. "Give service to your fellow men, even as a good king, and the vine will give you service. Give them death and it will give you—"

"Stop it!" Stobber shouted. "I don't want to hear any more of this damned nonsense. There ought to be a more reliable volume somewhere in this library. Let's keep looking."

Then Joe could hear the shuffling of books and the occasional scraping of feet. Their voices were conspicuously silent.

"Here's something," Stobber said finally. "When the lavender vine hangs itself upon the sun, great troubles will fall upon the land."

"That's nothing new," said Nitticello. "All the old timers quote that passage. And after all, what does it really mean? It never actually happens, does it?" The Prime Minister laughed at this. "How could the vine hang itself on a star that's millions of miles away. The vine is here on this planet. Right here under our palace."

"What if it has the ability to leave home, to leave our planet entirely," said Stobber. "People are seeing it everywhere these days. The slave masters have been seeing it all over the valley. And some of the Sashes claim that one arm of it has been hanging along the ledge under the new king's window—"

"S-s-s-sh. Someone's coming."

Joe listened intently. He heard a knock. It must have been one of the Sashes, he decided. Stobber beckoned him to enter. There was the sound of a door opening.

"I came to report something very strange, sir," a new voice said breathlessly.

"What is it?" Stobber snapped.

"The sun's coming up, sir—"

"Is there anything strange about that?"

"Well, sir, it looks like—like—" The new voice stammered and stopped.

"For heavens' sake, man—spit it out," the Prime Minister commanded.

"Well...it...it looks like the sun has turned purple, sir. I've never seen anything like it. The people in the streets are saying it's the vine, hanging in the air between the sun and us. But some of the old people are in a panic. They say it means catastrophe."

Joe's unintentional sharp breathing sent him gliding away once again, and the remainder of the conversation was lost.

CHAPTER TWENTY

JOE never knew when he went through the curve that reversed his direction, but he was surely falling up instead of down.

From somewhere out of the marshes he came through the surface, falling feet first—upward—into the open air.

He was half a mile high before he could realize that this was the same Karridonzan valley. Mentally he was still descending through the vine—until he discovered the rising sun.

He continued to fall upward. He was fountaining up through a shaft of the vein that couldn't be seen plainly in the sunlight. But wherever a shadow crossed it, from a wisp of cloud, it showed in clear-cut lines. It was like a geyser, Joe thought, rising through miles of air, straight toward the zenith.

He swung past a few scattered clouds, and then again he was within plain view of the sun. And there was more of the lavender vine! It was everywhere this morning. The whole countryside was alive with it.

"It hangs on the sun," he repeated. "There's a catastrophe ahead."

High over the valley he tried holding his breath to see whether he could stop his dizzy ride through what seemed to be only thin air. No, he was floating with just enough motion to cause the trees and buildings to turn gently, miles beneath him.

Now he began to descend.

He looked down to the red rectangles that comprised the palace roof far below. He tried to discern the ledge along one side of the building, wondering whether this particular arm of the vine would settle at that resting-place.

"There aren't any rules," he told himself. "It springs out of the mysterious depths of the planet in any quantity. It's like the wind. It grows until it's everywhere at once. It diminishes until it's nowhere. How can anyone ever control it?"

Many minutes passed before he realized that he was no longer falling. He was resting, high in the air, with nothing but an almost invisible trunk of light supporting him.

An air spinner from the skystation came across the purple mists and landed in the palace grounds. From this elevation Joe couldn't tell whether one person or many had arrived. He guessed that the visitor wouldn't stay long, for the spinner wasn't being wheeled into a hangar.

His curiosity began working. If the vine was going to hold him high up in the sky for an indefinite period, he fancied the idea of taking a brief nap. However, his desire to return to the palace seemed to start him in motion again—he was descending once more.

"Service!" He smiled to himself. No wonder Pudge was so

happy and carefree—for Pudge knew what it was to make a wish and have the vine obey.

There was just a moment of panic for Joe as he came down squarely over the roof of the palace. If he landed on the ledge, could he be sure the way was clear? Or would Nitticello and Stobber be right there waiting for him?

But Joe didn't land on the ledge. Instead, he moved gently and noiselessly right *through* the roof. It was amazing. The stones seemed to fold back and form an opening, which he dropped through within a few feet of a tall brick chimney. Ceilings and floors then made way for him through the upper levels of the palace in the same incredible manner. Then he slowed to a stop and found himself sitting on a heap of small objects in a dark room.

THE darkness caused him to squint for several moments, but when his eyes finally adjusted, he saw that a small amount of light came into the room from one miniature window no larger than a saucer. The window was a mosaic of glass that admitted a hundred little blades of colored light. And Joe suddenly realized that he was sitting on a heaped treasure of coins and precious stones.

Nitticello's private treasure, of course!

Joe gasped. His fingers touched the surfaces of coins all around him. He should have velvet gloves on, he thought. It was bewildering, unbelievable, untouchable. From the outlines of the room, he guessed that it would take more than a dozen large trunks to hold this collection. And here he was, sitting on top of it, barely able to contain himself.

What had the vine meant by dropping him into the middle of this incredible secret?

"Does King Arvo know about all this?" Joe muttered to himself. "What's Nitti been up to anyway?"

Even as he was gasping for understanding, he heard the slight thump of footsteps outside the thick wall.

A door opened very slowly. It was a thick metal door, and

Joe felt the swoosh of air before he saw the thin vertical crack of light.

Only two inches open, the door stopped. Nitti and a stranger were talking. The stranger, a thick-chested fellow in a dark green business suit, was trying to look in. Nitti wasn't quite ready for him to see.

"It's the same plan we've discussed many times before, Rouzey. If you can use serums to convert my slaves into controllable interplanetary mercenaries as you've always claimed you can, then I have enough treasure here for us to start things in motion."

Rouzey must have come from another planet, Joe thought. His voice was strange and metallic sounding. "Those I can't convert I can eliminate," Rouzey said. "We've already proved that part of it. But we can't get far, shaking down the whole interplanetary system unless we've got plenty of gems and gold to start with. As your man Stobber says, we'll need it for bait."

"That's the plan to this point." Nitticello opened the door another inch wider. "Are you ready to start?"

"As soon as you buy out the skystation. When that's done we'll have a respectable base where travelers pass."

"That will be easy," said Nitticello. "Things are already in place to "purchase" the new skystation office building." His inflection on the word purchase caused the stranger to laugh with a weird clang of his metallic throat.

Then Rouzey said, "All right. We have all the details settled. We'll be able to get a chokehold on as many as three or four planets before any of the big sleepy interstellar nations get wise—and by then it will be too late. But we've got to proceed carefully...smartly. Are you sure your king doesn't know you've made off with this wealth?"

The Prime Minister laughed. "That incompetent fool. I've kept him too busy bleeding the kingdom for taxes and stamping out slave trouble. He's not even aware that this vault exists."

"And you're sure he won't walk in on us?" Rouzey asked anxiously.

"Most certain, my dear Rouzey." Nitticello turned his head and made sure that Stobber had locked the outer door.

"All right," Rouzey said. "Let's see your treasure."

NITTICELLO swung the door open, and the light of the outer room glanced over the surfaces of gold and emerald and sapphire. The light also struck Joe full in the face.

"Ya-a-yaki-ying-yang!" Rouzey's immense chest shuddered like a wounded animal, and his copper gong throat gave out a wild series of notes. "The—the King!" he backed away.

"Nonsense." Nitti said huffily and started to walk in. He came in with a gun, and it was pointed in the only direction a gun could point in such a small narrow room. It would flash a ray straight through Joe's chest if he pulled the trigger. "Nonsense. I tell you the King is—"

Nitticello's elbows gave a backward jerk and his narrow eyes suddenly opened wide as if they meant to jump out of their sockets.

Joe jumped back, too. He bumped against the wall. He reached for a handful of the coins and gems. The only defense he could think of was to throw the stuff directly at the Prime Minister. He threw wild. There was a clang and a clatter and a spray of treasure through the door. It went wild because Joe wasn't fully under his own control. The vine still had him, and as he threw, the vine lifted him.

Click! Blaze! The stream of silver fire shot in from the ray pistol in the Prime Minister's hand—straight at Joe.

But the lavender vine seemed to catch the beam and splash it off. Invisible though the vine was, it was completely around Joe, holding him—and no ray could penetrate it. Pudge had told him that once before, and now he was seeing the proof.

He was rising…into the ceiling. How much had the Prime Minister actually seen?

Nitti was looking around blankly. "By heavens there's no one in there now," he said with shaky confidence. "Not a soul." he pocketed his gun.

"I swear I saw the King. It was the King!" Rouzey said, coming back to the door.

"It must have been an optical illusion," said Nitti, looking as pale as white gold. "It had to be. You can see for yourself no one's there."

"What made those coins come flying out?" Rouzey grated.

"Oh, that? That always happens when we open the door. Dust combustion or some such thing. Isn't that right, Stobber?"

Joe heard Stobber give an irritated cough. "Sure, it always happens. Er…excuse me, Nitti, I'm going below just to make sure the King's still where we think he is."

Then Joe was going up again, and the opening through the palace roof was closing after him. He'd have to tell Pudge about all this. But by the stars and comets, he was going to think twice before he made another wish that the lavender vine might fulfill.

CHAPTER TWENTY-ONE

ACROSS the brown and green valley toward the western edge of the kingdom, the battle had begun. It began as many civil wars begin, with a trifling incident between citizens and authorities. A tradesman was confronted by one of the Sashes and asked to give certain information that he didn't possess. The Sash had been drinking, contrary to court regulations, and he forgot that he wasn't speaking to a slave. He grew arrogant when the tradesman couldn't answer him, and struck the fellow across the hand with a whip. The tradesman turned on him and threatened to strike him. The Sash gave him two more lashes, and by that time a crowd had gathered. People weren't used to seeing a law-abiding tradesman in trouble.

"Don't strike back," someone yelled at him. But the tradesman was seeing red. He picked up a nearby carpenter's tool—a mallet—and struck the Sash on the side of the head.

Two more Sashes came up to establish order, but a score of townsmen had already rushed to the defense of their fellow citizen, and the battle was on.

Seven persons, including two women, were sliced through with ray fire, and that escalated the event into a mushrooming battle. The town's alarm bells rang. People came running from all the surrounding neighborhoods. When certain slave masters refused to join the mob, the townsmen pushed them into the street, toward the barricade of vehicles that the defending Sashes had hastily put together.

By evening, the ringleaders of the skirmish were joined by other rebel groups from neighboring towns who came pouring in after hearing the news of their fellow citizens' deaths.

Within hours, violence against the King's Sashes was spreading to other villages and townships. In many villages local officials rode up and down the streets shouting frantically from loud speakers for everyone to go home and stay there and not to join the outbreak. But that wasn't enough to stop the tide. The dam had burst.

When morning came, Nadoff led an advance through the streets of Redroot Hill. Eight hundred slaves dropped their jobs and joined the march.

They moved eastward. It was a badly organized army, almost entirely without firearms. Events had happened so quickly there hadn't been enough time to procure weaponry with the money obtained by the sale of the royal jewels. How ironic that seemed to Nadoff. He ordered a small detail to take some of the funds and purchase food and medical supplies from villages not yet affected by the uprising.

"These men will need to eat hearty if they're to maintain their strength in battle. Bring back as much as you can," he told the detail leader. "Take whatever vehicles you can and join us at nightfall."

The rebels continued to march. The slaves picked up clubs along the way, or brought pitchforks, or gathered sacks of rocks. Some of the townsmen who joined them carried ray pistols. A few of them had cars. The cars moved along slowly, matching the speed of the marching army that accompanied them. Slowly but surely they were moving toward the palace at the far side of the kingdom.

That forenoon the air spinners from the palace arsenal attacked them.

The air spinners were deadly. They flew in low and used their ray guns to strafe the advancing throngs of rebels and automobiles. The attacks left many of the cars crippled and useless—and there were many casualties.

But the rebels by this time had taken to the shelter of the many thick groves of trees that hugged the ridge road to the palace, both above and below it. Though the running battle was becoming more fierce, the rebels kept making progress, not backward but forward.

"It's Nitticello's neck or ours!" That seemed to be the common battle cry.

It was lucky, Joe thought, that they seemed to have largely forgiven the King and were venting their wrath against the Prime Minister. Gradually the word circulated through the ranks that the King was actually on the side of the rebellion.

And the word spread quickly:

"The King is on our side, he's one of us."

"Nitticello tried to assassinate him."

"The King is marching somewhere within our own ranks."

"There's going to be a showdown between the King and the Prime Minister."

All this and more circulated across the kingdom like wildfire.

THE effect of the scuttlebutt was profound, and it helped lift and maintain the spirits of the men who were marching for their freedom. They knew that somewhere among them was their king…a king who wore slave clothes and was marching in a mob against the evils of his own land.

Joe had joined the advancing army within the first hour of the battle. The lavender vine having deposited him back on the ground. He too had discarded his kingly clothes in favor of a slave outfit. But he carried a bundle containing a blue uniform with gold epaulettes, just in case. Also a trim mustache and a spade shaped beard that might be added to his make-up at a moment's notice.

By the second morning he found Marcia, who was traveling in one of the rebel cars with a family. The driver of the car was the Karridonzan woman whose voice he had heard while whirling down the shaft of the lavender vine.

"You'll have to leave the car," Joe advised, stopping them on the ridge road at daybreak. He and the King had been helping Nadoff stand watch during the latter part of the night.

"Joe!" Marcia exclaimed. "You're with us, aren't you?"

"Of course I am, but this is no time to talk," Joe snapped. "Drive into the thicket if you want to save the car. There'll be air spinners over us before the sun shows—"

The sun was coming up, and it was again shrouded by the arteries of the lavender vine hanging above the mist. A moment later the air spinners were seen rising into the sky.

Joe jumped into the car, taking control of the vehicle. He shot ahead over the road and then swung down over the ridge through a break in the wooded slope. The car jumped a ravine, careened, righted itself, and plunged deep into the darkness of the woods. Another ravine was ahead, too deep to cross. Marcia screamed.

"Stop, Joe!" Marcia cried.

Joe slammed on the brakes—his foot all the way to the floor. He was crashing against branches. But there was a ravine, and that was what he wanted. He steered into it, and the car jerked and clunked to a stop.

He swung the door open.

"Quick…under the car—everybody!"

It was a fast scramble. Marcia was beside him, then the woman and the others. Now the ray fire was slicing the treetops away. An air spinner went past in a hurry, and all through the forested area you heard the swishing and crashing of treetops falling.

Everyone along the ridge had ducked for the lowest point.

The luckiest ones were protected—as Marcia and her party were—from things that fell from overhead.

"Here they come again," Joe warned. "Stay where you are."

"Joe," Marcia was holding tight to his arm. He caught her hand.

"They're not going to get us, pal," Joe said. "Even if they do, the rest of the army will keep on marching. This is it."

"I'm not scared," she said, "I just wanted to say thanks…thanks for coming."

The air spinners found many targets that morning and there were some severe losses. But the rebel army still marched on, gathering more recruits everywhere it went. There was a great relief among the ranks, though, when nightfall finally came.

"It's Nitticello's neck or ours," the hushed battle cry continued.

By this time the King's identity and precarious situation was fully known among the men. In fact it was King Arvo himself who circulated the story that they couldn't lose the rebellion because they had not one, but two kings on their side. Joe Peterson, the American slave, then became known as the second "King." The account of Joe's saving the real King from the Prime Minister's assassination scheme spread quickly through the ranks.

"And it was the American girl's jewels that bought our dinner tonight," some of the self-appointed captains announced as the rebel throngs passed the supply cars to be served their midnight meals.

THE searchlights from three air spinners played over the valley, trying to locate the rebel encampment. At one point a bright beam swept over Joe and the rest of the inner circle that had gathered around Nadoff. The flash of the King's blue uniform with the gold trimmings showed for just an instant. Joe had turned the uniform over to him and, with Nadoff's consent, the King had restored himself to his original appearance. A careful shave, after several days of growing whiskers, had brought back the trim pattern of his mustache and beard. He looked fine, Joe thought—more regal than ever. And the passing searchlight gave Joe a reassuring glimpse. Here was a moment of danger, but there seemed to be a new strength in the King's face.

"You may be right about Arvo," Joe whispered to Marcia. "He may possess the qualities that Karridonza needs in a king."

"I hope he'll have the chance to show them."

Nadoff, who had been listening, joined in on the conversation. "I hope so to. You know it was very hard for me at first to believe he was the real King—and then it was even harder for me to put any measure of trust in him. We had all despised him for so many years. However, I believe your instincts are right about him, Miss Melinda. He may be just the person—perhaps the only person—who can lead our kingdom out of oppression. Has it occurred to you, my dear, that he might need the strength of a good woman at his side? Karridonza could use a beautiful queen like you."

Joe tried to read her expression by starlight. Her answer was evasive.

"There's some work I must attend to with the food supplies," she said, rising. "If you'll excuse me please, gentlemen." Then she looked in Joe's direction. "We'll see each other again before we reach the palace."

A little later that night Joe and King Arvo came up with a bold plan of action, and with Nadoff's consent, they attempted to communicate with the lavender vine.

Like a stationary bolt of lightning skirting the tops of the trees, it came into view—deep purple turning to blue and then to brilliant lavender. It was an incredible sight, and it was less than half a mile away.

Arvo expressed concern. "I hope no one is under the vine— it could mean their death."

Joe knew the King was terribly upset over the way the vine had caused recent chance disasters.

"When it flows over the country on an errand, I'm always

afraid it will strike innocent victims."

"That's what happened the first two nights I saw it," said Joe. "But after that, the frog boy and I began to use it without any such trouble. I don't understand it."

"There are many secrets to controlling it," the King said. "If we're going to make use of it, we've got to work together—you and I—along with all the rest. We've got to all wish for the same thing—that's the key."

"That should be easy," Nadoff said. "What we all want is a showdown with Nitticello."

"If you'll call the leaders together," King Arvo said, "I'll reveal what I know about handling the vine. Then, if luck is with us, it may move over to the ridge and pick us up bodily and take us right to the palace door."

Joe and Nadoff's jaws dropped upon hearing this.

The King continued, smiling. "We'll turn our march into a joyride."

The vine was moving slowly now, coming closer, but moving uncertainly. It was near enough that Joe could see the flow of light through the trunk and out into the undulating branches. There was a huge claw tonight, as there had been the night it had picked him up at the wrecked air spinner. Joe shuddered. After all the amazingly delightful rides he had taken, he shouldn't have any fears. But there was an angry look about the claw—gigantic fingers of light.

"It could strike down a hundred Sashes," someone had said hopefully at its first appearance. But now that same observer was saying, "It could slap down a thousand slaves."

A tremble of panic was going through the rebel army. Joe wondered whether it had been a mistake to call the vine into service.

The leaders gathered close around Nadoff, the King, and Joe. It was a moment for King Arvo to prove that he was truly willing to share his deepest secrets.

The King began.

"It isn't easy to give away a secret if the secret is so complicated that one has to live with it and work with it before he knows it intimately himself. I believe the rash acts and unaccountable deaths caused by the vine can be attributed to the fact that the Prime Minister and myself were not in harmony. Our wishes were never in balance. And although I have made many mistakes, I know that my greatest mistake was that of yielding to Nitticello—time and time again. When he tried to command the vine, his wishes were always more selfish than mine. And that always gave the vine a strong countenance of anger."

"It looks angry tonight," Joe said.

The crowd, standing in the darkness, their faces dimly lighted by the flare of lavender, kept turning to watch. The vine was moving around them gradually.

"Better hurry," Nadoff said. "Tell us what to do."

"I can't hurry," Arvo said, "because the vine isn't ready for a command—not until all of you understand. You see, the vine knows us. It's a power in our lives. And what does it do to us? Here is the secret: It gives back to us what we give to others."

The King paused. There were whisperings among the men before he continued.

"For those of you who give your neighbors kindliness, the vine will give back kindliness. Sometimes the return gift takes a freakish form. A little boy at the court who was always playing mischief upon others received a gift of mischief from the vine. It gave him some of the characteristics of a frog. This American slave who helped us out of the mud—who gave us a lift—has been given many a lift by the vine. Am I right, Joe Peterson?"

"Y—yes," Joe answered. "So that's it. I'm beginning to understand these favors. But go on. What about this business of being susceptible to change? The frog-boy was telling me—"

"That's very important for us to know. If the vine lifts us, as we hope, and takes us to the door of the palace so we can have our showdown with Nitticello, there'll be a crucial moment for every one of us. After being in the hands of the vine, our natures are ready to bend more easily than at other times. The frog-boy received his frog nature when he played in the swamp after a ride in the vine. And my friend, Joe Peterson, confesses that he felt himself turning into a king—almost—as the result of a secret wish that was strong in him after a ride on the vine."

"Then what are we to wish for?" Nadoff asked.

"If the vine will engulf us, we'll descend from it wishing that we may all be proud, honest citizens—and free."

"It's coming," someone shouted.

"Don't be afraid," Arvo called out. "Ascend the ridge and wait. And wish, first of all, for a showdown with Nitticello."

Joe joined the hike, trying to keep an eye on Arvo. He was proud of the things Arvo had said. But he couldn't help being a little jealous, too, for Marcia was right, the King had qualities Karridonza needed. If he succeeded in regaining his thrown— and if he was indeed infatuated with Marcia—how could Joe stand in the way of her becoming his queen?

They were gathered on the ridge, under the stars. The angry edged fingers of the vine began to hop swiftly back and forth through a half-mile semi-circle.

"Wish!" the King called out to the men.

A score of responses all cried the same words: "We're wishing!"

To Joe's utter amazement, the vine began to retreat. It struck off across the Karridonzan valley like a runaway.

"Where's it going?"

"It will come back," the King said confidently. "It's never been known to cross the purple mists."

But as they watched, Joe saw that it did cross the mists. It went out of sight on the distant horizon, in the direction of the skystation.

For a long moment they watched in silence. Then Nadoff said, "We'd better get back into the woods. It will soon be daylight, and some air spinner will catch us here."

"No, we'll wait here," King Arvo said quietly. "Keep wishing."

CHAPTER TWENTY-TWO

JOE thought King Arvo had lost control. Nadoff started down the slope, and as the word spread to the rest of the group, Joe knew that they were all going to leave.

"Seevia...Seevia..." the King muttered.

"It's coming back!" Joe shouted. "Stay here with the King. The vine is coming back!"

Nadoff turned. Everyone could see it now. So they waited, all of them sharing the same thoughts, all of them wishing for the same thing.

"Seevia...Seevia...Seevia..." The King's chant was lost in the excited jumble of voices. Yes, the vine was whirling back like a luminous inverted twister. There was angry power in it, Joe thought. It whipped over the purple mist, raced down into the valley, and leaped over villages.

The fingers weren't visible. Perhaps they were lost in the whirl; or they were transparent in the early morning sunlight. But many branches could be seen, flaring out like lightning, then jumping back to spin around the central stem.

"It's bringing something!" King Arvo shouted. "Something huge."

The vine seemed to be carrying something quite large, but it was concealed within its upper reaches. None of the men could make out exactly what it was, but whatever it was, it was tremendous in size.

Within a mile of the men it slowed its pace. Now it glided over the ground between them and the fortress. It seemed to be trying to guide them. King Arvo and Nadoff both noticed this.

"Follow the vine...it's leading us."

As they began marching in the direction of the vine, Joe called out to the King.

"We might be able to use it like a smoke screen. Rays can't penetrate it."

They followed the vine for some time. It was a long, tedious two-hour march, even with the vine's protection against the rays. For no one succeeded in getting into the vine until it had come to rest within two hundred yards of the palace.

But through those two hours of marching, it continually screened them from destruction, and three times it shot out an angry arm at approaching air spinners. At one point, three of the spinners whirled about and attacked again.

Flash!

One of the spinners went hurtling downward. There was an earth-shaking crash and a huge ball of fire. The other two spinners sped away in search of healthier skies.

"The vine is still carrying something," Arvo kept repeating. It still wasn't clear what the object was. The vine seemed to be trying to conceal it from view. "It must have picked up something quite large on the other side of the mists."

The palace ray guns were slicing the earth from the top of the ridge on either side of the lavender vine. The air was streaked with red and silver lines. Stobber and his Sashes were making things hot for them now. They moved ahead under great difficulty. Tree tops jumped. Hilltops leaped from their bases. Sprays of dirt bounced and splattered, but through the clouds of dust the rebel army advanced.

"Keep back of the vine!" Nadoff yelled. "Watch it! It's going over the ridge."

Joe bounded over the ridge, then stopped, crouching, while the hundreds of others rushed up to take a new position. The rays from the spinners were quick death for anyone who couldn't leap fast enough, and many men were lost every time the vine swerved for a new position. Joe was glad he had persuaded Marcia to remain hidden with the women at the night's encampment. However, when the palace was finally captured, he knew that she and the others would soon be with them again.

"Look!" King Arvo cried. "It's going to drop its load—get back—everyone!"

The huge twisted lavender stem was so large that its vibrating roots covered half of the two hundred yards that now separated the small ridge from the palace. It was settling down now, a massive lavender cylinder of light, right at the edge of the execution grounds.

There it deposited its load…

A building.

It was the handsome new skyscraper from the Karridonza skystation! The vine had literally picked the building up in one piece and carried it back to transplant it in front of the royal palace.

Joe watched the lavender fingers cut away the ground beneath; he saw the swirling trunk exert its mighty pressure as the building settled down into place. No ray could touch it. The swirl of lavender grew thinner, but it was still there, spiraling its screen of safety. Under the forenoon sun it showed as a thin pinkish haze. The white building within its whirl reflected its tinted light.

"Now!" King Arvo cried. "Into the building. Your new fortress awaits you. Come on, men!"

CHAPTER TWENTY-THREE

THE rebel army flowed into the building. It was a godsend and they knew it. They filled its lobby, clamoring for orders. What would be next? How would they proceed with their attack?

Nadoff held his head. The clamor was too much for him. The slaves were racing from one room to another, jubilant. They shouted with joy, as if a victory had already been won. Their sweat and toil had given many a new building to Karridonza, and the lavender vine appeared to be returning the favor. It was theirs—this beautiful building. And it was wonderful.

Joe tried to shout them down.

"Quiet, you men…you're in danger! The vine won't stay here long. As soon as it goes, the ray guns will chop this structure down to the ground! Quiet! *Quiet!*"

Nadoff found the King and put a microphone before him. The loud speaker silenced the shouting.

"Listen to me!" Arvo commanded. "This is a surprise on all of us. We didn't ask for this. It just came. All we asked for was a showdown with Nitticello and his defenders. And we know they are in the palace, with all of the weapons of the fortress at their command. Why the lavender vine brought us this building from the skystation I can't say. But I believe the vine is on our side. And as long as it doesn't leave us exposed to the rays, this is our fortress."

The rebel army cheered. Joe shuddered. They were feeling too confident.

"Now," King Arvo spoke loudly to the men, "Nadoff and I have a plan. We'll send four squads from four directions to break into the palace and kidnap the Prime Minister. I know the entry ports well. It's a gamble, but if we can bring him back safely, we'll force Nitticello to radio Stobber and his men, commanding them to stop—"

King Arvo's speech was interrupted by a cry from the wide curved stairs in one corner of the wide lobby.

"Nitticello is here—in the building. I saw him."

It was a girl's voice—Marcia Melinda's. Yes, it was she, disguised as a townsman. She had marched with the rebel army after all.

"Where did you see him?" Arvo shouted.

"He was up here on the balcony the minute we entered. He ran up to the next floor. I followed him up to make sure it was really him. He ran further on up the stairwell, looking for a place to hide."

So the vine had answered the wish. Joe saw it plainly now. They had wanted a showdown with Nitticello. But Nitti wasn't at the palace. He had made off to the skystation to buy the headquarters he needed for his scheme with Rouzey. But the vine had gone after him. It had cleared the building of everyone but Nitticello, and then it had lifted him—building and all—and brought him back to face the rebel army.

"Come down from there, Marcia Melinda," the King cried. He was breaking a path through the mob, marching toward the stairs. Joe was beating a trail in the same direction.

Ahead of them, eighteen or twenty slaves bounded up the curved stairway waving clubs and knives. They meant to find the Prime Minister.

"You men stop!" King Arvo shouted. "Come back down here—this is my fight."

Before any of the men could obey, a volley of shots sounded from the other side of the lobby. The Sashes were pouring in.

From then on, it became a free-for-all. Clubs and knives and pitchforks against whips, knives and ray pistols—but to the slaves' amazement, none of the ray pistols seemed to be working. The Sashes moved in, intending to mow the rebel army down with a scythe of ray fire, but none of their guns worked...

They were within the vine—their guns were dead.

When the Sashes realized what was happening, they started to back away in a slow retreat. The wide entrance to the building was jammed, though, because other Sashes were pushing in from behind. The plan for a quick, devastating attack by the Prime Minister's guards was crumbling.

Clang! Clack! Clatter!

The Sashes were suddenly throwing their pistols right and left, but they tried to fight on with swords and whips.

NADOFF had been fighting near King Arvo when he suddenly climbed onto a large shelf mounted on the wall. Seizing a statuette, he hurled it at the advancing Sashes. A moment later he dodged a flying knife—and he literally laughed in the faces of his enemy. King Arvo and Joe Peterson couldn't believe what they were seeing.

The ring of Nadoff's laugh reverberated above the din, and it was enough to make his slave followers rush even more into the fray of battle. *Clang! Crash! Thump!* It was total pandemonium throughout the wide marble-walled lobby.

Joe struck down three Sashes on his way to the stairs. He wanted Nitticello. Nitti's thousands of crimes pounded through his mind. The inexcusable beatings. The constant robberies. The interplanetary plots. Murders and more murders—and two near murders that had been foiled only by fate…King Arvo and Marcia Melinda.

Where was Marcia?

She must have led a squad of slaves up the stairs to find the Prime Minister.

Joe reached the balcony. He raced up the next flight. Three slaves lay in the corridor. Two were dying. The third, clutching his arm, was writhing in pain.

"Nitticello?" Joe cried.

"Up there," the slave groaned. "He's armed with a large hypodermic needle."

Joe sprung up the next flight. He dodged two more casualties on the stairs. Then he hit the top landing and saw the Prime Minister.

It was Nitticello—and Marcia!

The Prime Minister was truly in his element. Even from a side angle Joe could see the evil in his face. You could see it in the way he moved stealthily toward his intended victim. Marcia was trapped at the end of the corridor and Nitticello was advancing slowly toward her, clasping the hypodermic needle—making ready.

Marcia's eyes were wide with terror. She didn't scream, though. Perhaps she couldn't.

At the sound of Joe's running steps the Prime Minister whirled. Joe lunged for him. Nitticello swung with the needle. Joe caught his arm, though, and threw it aside. The needle went flying and literally jammed into the wall. Joe tore into him with a body block that sent them both spinning to the floor.

The Prime Minister was no match for Joe, and the struggle might have ended quickly if Marcia hadn't rushed into the fray armed with a short, heavy wooden club. She took a full swung just as the two struggled to their feet. The blow missed the Prime Minister but caught Joe across the side of the head. He saw dancing comets. Nitticello made a mad dash as Joe crumbled to the floor. Marcia was beside herself.

"Joe! Joe!" She grabbed him by the shoulders and shook him. "Lord, what have I done! Come out of it, Joe—he's getting away!"

Marcia commenced slapping Joe's cheeks. He stared blankly for a moment. The floor and walls were still weaving, but he knew he had to get to his feet.

"Did he get you?" Joe mumbled.

"No. I'm all right. But if you hadn't come—" She was breathless, tugging at his arm. He finally managed to pull himself up. He blinked his eyes hard and shook his head. He could see the needle in the wall, but Nitticello was nowhere in sight.

"Nitti…where is he?"

"This way…quick," Marcia cried. "He's trying to go up to the next floor, but the door at the top of the stairs is solid—it's locked. I tried it already. We can trap him there if we hurry."

However, Nitticello had already encountered the locked door. He bolted back down the stairs and sprang into the corridor again. His eyes flashed a look of near insanity as he gave Joe a momentary glare. Then he reversed course and bounded down the opposite stairwell.

The chase went on and on—down another flight, then another—over the bodies of Nitti's victims and down the last curving flight toward the lobby. Joe was at his heels, Marcia followed close behind.

Strangely, the free-for-all in the lobby had come nearly to a dead stop. For an instant Joe couldn't understand why. Sashes and rebels alike were staring at the high lobby ceiling as if hypnotized. Then, as he neared the bottom of the stairs, Joe saw. The hazy lavender light had thickened along the upper walls and gathered into a clearly visible claw overhead—coiled fingers of the vine. They glowed with a ghastly pink light. They were curved like immense steel hooks. The back of the lavender hand moved slowly beneath the ceiling. The great fingers twitched as if ready to pounce.

UNDER this spell it was no wonder that the whole roomful of chaos had frozen into a tableau of terror. Nitticello, sensing the threat from above, stopped abruptly at the bottom of the stairs. Joe and Marcia held back, and Joe's heart skipped a beat as he gauged the anger in the hovering vine. But there was Nitticello—right below him. Joe moved slowly down the last few steps toward the Prime Minister— his fists tight.

"No, Joe!" Marcia called. "Stop!"

Then Marcia did something unexpected. Everyone in the lobby saw what she did. With a quick movement, she tossed her club out into the lobby toward a figure in a regal blue uniform with gold epaulettes.

"To his majesty, King Arvo!" She sang out the challenge, and every Sash and rebel and slave understood. It was to be a fight to the finish between the Prime Minister and the King.

Joe saw Arvo's eyes flash as he caught the club in mid-air air. The lavender claw held back, waiting. The men in the lobby made way for the King as he moved toward the Prime Minister.

Nitti stood at the bottom of the steps, he reached down and grabbed a club off the floor and waited for the King. But fear was in his eyes. Suddenly he dropped the club and folded his arms with that wonderful poise of his. Joe saw his face tighten with the old lines of arrogance.

"Your majesty..." Nitticello said, giving a slight bow. "You've made a serious mistake. But I can help you out of it."

"I've made no mistake this time," Arvo said through clenched teeth. He kept advancing, his steps measured.

But the Prime Minister meant to play the old game again— what else could he do? It was his last hope. "Don't do anything you'll regret Arvo. Let's talk this over."

That was a smooth line, Joe thought. Would it work again?

"No regrets here," said Arvo. "I'm simply going to beat the life out of you, Nitticello, and there'll be no regrets."

"Wait…Arvo…your majesty!" Terror broke into the Prime Minister's voice. "If you have grievances against me, I'll listen. Give me the opportunity to defend myself. Don't be traitorous toward your own Prime Minister."

"The people of Karridonza may judge who is traitorous."

No rebel could have marched against a foe with a more convincing show of righteous indignation. Arvo raised his club to strike. And Joe was proud of him, for he knew Arvo would never succumb to illicit pressure again.

The club was almost ready to swing when Nitticello screeched, "Look out…the vine!"

It might have been a last trick, but it wasn't. Joe saw the angry lavender fingers swoop down from the ceiling. They pierced down between the King and the Prime Minister. They stiffened and glided toward Nitticello. He backed away in horror. The fingers followed—and Arvo followed—and after him came the whole lobby full of rebels and Sashes, determined to see this clash to the finish.

The lavender fingers forced the Prime Minister out the lobby door. It was a moving drama followed by an audience that was virtually hypnotized.

"Let them fight it out!" Joe cried.

Joe looked back and saw a nod of agreement from Marcia. If wishes could have controlled the vine in that tense moment, the King would surely have had his chance to put a quick end to the kingdom's oppressor.

And he meant to. He bit his words savagely. "You can't escape me now, Nitti. The vine is on my side."

Nitticello flung back. "You're lying. The vine is protecting me. It has always protected me. I know all the secrets."

"Then you know that the vine gives back what you give to others." Arvo advanced into the sunshine beyond the lobby door. The thin fingers of lavender still separated them as

Nitticello backed away. "What have you given to others, Nitticello? Death? The vine will gladly give it back to you."

IT was the thick surly voice of Stobber, chief of the Sashes, that shouted an obscene taunt in answer to the King's words. Joe hadn't seen him, but he must have been waiting outside of the building, directing his Sashes from a position of safety. Now he stepped into the opening in front of the crowd and began shooting.

The ray pistol worked!

He shot into the rebel group indiscriminately, and cut a swath of death through their foreranks. Now that the vine had gathered into a claw, it had left an unprotected space beneath— enough space for pistol fire.

Nine slaves and townsmen melted away under Stobber's quick blast. Nadoff fell to the ground, but Joe was sure the beams had missed him. Sashes and slaves alike were electrified by this action. Pistols worked again! There would have been an instantaneous stampede for discarded pistols if—in the next split second—the lavender vine hadn't taken the violence into its own angry hands.

The claw of the vine leaped and seized Stobber. It caught him by the handsome green and orange mane over the top of his head and lifted him off the ground. The ray gun went dead again.

"Stobber!" Nitticello cried. The vine's fingers no longer protected him and the King was after him. "Stobber! Help me. *Help* me!"

Stobber was being lifted, though, and Nitticello ran to him and grabbed his feet, trying to pull him down. The claw of the vine was rising. The Prime Minister held on. He was kicking wildly but was afraid to let go. Then he wasn't *able* to let go— the vine had both of them.

The two of them were carried, kicking and screaming, over the King's station in the center of the execution grounds. The vine began to lower them. Nitticello's dangling feet accidentally kicked against the red handle at the upper end of the blue metal bar. Joe wondered if any of the red came off on Nitti's boot.

A moment later the lavender claw lowered into the chamber. The two men, swaying like a lavender pendulum, went down into the disintegration machine.

The invisible walls of disintegration rays moved in from both sides and sliced away at the human pendulum. The crowd hushed. Everyone saw what was happening. Nitticello and Stobber screamed in total horror for a few moments, then were silent. They dissolved swiftly. Within a minute or two there was nothing left but the crest of Stobber's skull with the green and orange mane—the handle by which he had been held. This remaining bit of Stobber was still caught in the vine's grip as the whole tower of lavender light rose slowly and drifted up into the sunshine—over the ridge and out across the valley. When Joe last saw it, the vine appeared to be lowering and dissolving above the marshes.

"This will be a new beginning for Arvo," Joe whispered to Marcia as they watched in awe from the edge of the crowd.

"Yes," Marcia said, "He's won his right to be king."

"He's won his right to practically anything he wants," Joe said stonily, not looking at Marcia…

CHAPTER TWENTY-FOUR

A few hours later King Arvo stood at the window of one of his palace rooms, talking into the telephone. His Prime Minister had called.

"Yes, Mr. Prime Minister. Are you getting settled?"

The voice on the other end was Nadoff.

"I'm already feeling much at home in my new office, your majesty."

Arvo looked across the grounds to the new skyscraper less than a hundred yards distant. The building had recently been purchased with the King's funds, Arvo had learned, and although the late Nitticello hadn't planned that it would be moved into the shadow of the King's fortress, here it was—and here it would stay. Arvo could see the round form of Nadoff in one of the upper story windows, telephoning from his new Prime Minister's quarters.

"Have you prepared the statement I commissioned?" Arvo asked.

"I have it outlined, your majesty. There are four main points. One—abolish all slavery. Two—test the Sashes for loyalty, retaining the best of them and purging the rest. Three—refill their ranks with the worthiest and most qualified of ex-slaves. And finally, four—take whatever steps necessary to assure the kingdom that the lavender vine will never again strike recklessly."

"Good enough," said the King. "I'll check with you later on the fine details of the draft."

"I beg to report, your majesty, that my first official caller was here—a frog-creature."

"Pudge? The little frog-boy? What in the world did he want from you?"

"He wishes to offer the palace a souvenir as a symbol of his good will. He brought the green and orange mane of Stobber, which he found in the swamp."

King Arvo chuckled. "All right. Tell him we'll accept. In fact, we'll grant him a favor in return. Find out if there's anything he wants."

"There is, your majesty. He hopes he may join the chants around the nine lanterns without being beaten for it."

"Grant him his wish, Nadoff. And tell him also that we'll add a tenth lantern in the row in his special honor. Is he there now?"

"No, sire. He disappeared quite mysteriously shortly after my conference with him."

"All well and good," Arvo said, smiling. "I think he already knows our decision." At that moment Arvo saw a pair of large green eyes peeking around one of the marble pillars, and now he heard a little froggish chortle from that direction.

Nadoff was still on the phone, though. "There's another matter of business that needs to come to your attention, your majesty. I find that one of your former court guests is quite anxious to return to her native planet. A beautiful Earth girl by the name of—"

"Marcia..." Arvo said in a low breath. "Yes, of course."

"I discouraged her," said Nadoff, "on the grounds that you might possibly have a plan for her—or am I presuming too much?"

"Please send her to me at once," Arvo said. "I want to talk with her personally."

A short time later Marcia arrived at the palace. When, she entered, the King welcomed her warmly and walked with her, arm in arm, into an ornate conference room.

"So you wish to go back to your native planet, Miss Melinda—Marcia?"

"Yes, your majesty—Arvo."

HE handed her a small ivory jewel box. She opened it, and it contained a lovely string of pearls. "I'll be honored if you accept them, with the compliments of Karridonza."

"Thank you, Arvo." her eyes were shining.

He paced in front of the table, then turned to her. The longer speech he had wanted to make suddenly melted to a few blunt words. "You've played an important part in the destiny of Karridonza, my dear. And we'll never forget you for it."

"And you, Arvo—your *majesty*—" she was smiling and her words were tumbling with emotion, "I'm so glad I've stayed long enough to see you win back your people—and your courage. You've proved that your rightful place is on the throne. You've changed so much for the better—"

"Yes...yes thanks to the lavender vine, and Nadoff, and Joe—and you. But though I've won my people back, I haven't yet won everyone."

"Haven't you?"

He came to her and took her hand.

"You don't have to leave, my dear Marcia. There's no law against your staying. And if there is, I'll change it with the stroke of a pen. You might like our world well enough to—to marry and settle down."

Marcia was shaking her head. "Thank you, Arvo. You are a wonderful man—but I truly need to return home."

"Soon?"

"There's a space ship leaving at midnight."

King Arvo gave her a little wink. "I thought it might work out this way." He looked away for a moment, a thoughtful expression on his face, then he smiled. "Very well. I'd better send an escort with you, though. After all, it's an old Karridonzan custom."

"A slave?"

"An ex-slave. There are no slaves in Karridonza anymore, as you well know." Arvo moved toward the marble columns and called a name.

"Joe."

Joe Peterson strolled into the room, trying to appear casual. Marcia looked at him as if to shame him. "Oh, an eavesdropper…"

"I always keep a double around in case of an emergency," the King interjected. "Joe Peterson, are you willing to accompany Miss Melinda as far as the skystation?"

Joe laughed. "Stop this farce—both of you." He walked up and looked directly into the Earth woman's eyes. "Marcia, I believe I know what you feel in your heart for me. And I *know* you know how I feel about you." He gave a slight bow. "With your permission, I've already bargained with the King to marry us here in the palace—right now if you like. This way I can escort all the way to Earth."

Marcia swallowed her smile and tried hard to look offended. "You two have taken advantage of me. Don't I have anything to say about this?"

"You're doomed," Joe said, drawing her into his arms. "Any

last request?"

Her stern look gave way to a happy glow. "One last request, Joe. Ask his majesty to tie the knot with a bit of lavender vine, so it will bring us back again some day."

THE END